SO-BHW-890

Desire

Desire

HUGO CLAUS

Translated by Stacey Knecht

Viking

VIKING
Published by the Penguin Group
Penguin Putnam Inc., 375 Hudson Street,
New York, New York 10014, U.S.A.
Penguin Books Ltd, 27 Wrights Lane,
London W8 5TZ, England
Penguin Books Australia Ltd, Ringwood,
Victoria, Australia
Penguin Books Canada Ltd, 10 Alcorn Avenue,
Toronto, Ontario, Canada M4V 3B2
Penguin Books (N.Z.) Ltd, 182–190 Wairau Road,
Auckland 10, New Zealand

Penguin Books Ltd, Registered Offices:
Harmondsworth, Middlesex, England

First published in 1997 by Viking Penguin,
a member of Penguin Putnam Inc.

10 9 8 7 6 5 4 3 2 1

Originally published in Dutch under the title
Het Verlangen by De Bezige Bij, Amsterdam.

LIBRARY OF CONGRESS CATALOGING-IN-PUBLICATION DATA
Claus, Hugo, 1929–
    [Verlangen. English]
    Desire / Hugo Claus ; translated by Stacey Knecht.
    p. cm.
    ISBN 0-670-86746-2 (alk. paper)
    I. Knecht, Stacey.
    PT6410.C553C3813   1997
    839.3'1364—dc21   97-22190

This book is printed on acid-free paper.
∞
Printed in the United States of America
Set in Janson text
Designed by Sabrina Bowers

And he removed from thence, and digged another well; and for that they strove not: and he called the name of it Rehoboth; and he said, For now the Lord hath made room for us, and we shall be fruitful in the land.

—Genesis 26:22

And he dreamed, and behold a ladder set up on the earth, and the top of it reached to heaven: and behold the angels of God ascending and descending on it.

—Genesis 28:12

And Jacob kissed Rachel, and lifted up his voice, and wept.

—Genesis 29:11

And Jacob heard that Schechem had defiled Dinah his daughter.

—Genesis 34

Desire

I

WHY THE UNICORN IS NEARLY FULL by half past nine in the morning? It certainly isn't the charms of Marta, the owner, or because Patrick, her husband, is so droll, or generous, or debonair. Forget it! Those two are a couple of nigglers and no mistake.

The whole thing's Rickabone's fault. Or should we say, the late departed Rickabone. Before his time this would've been unthinkable. Some mornings it'd be going on eleven and not a soul in the Unicorn, not a blessed flea, unless you counted the ones on Mister Jules, Patrick's dachshund, a bald smelly mutt that was too bone-lazy to lift his head when the bell rang and a traveling salesman walked in but would start yelping and gasping and wriggling like he had the falling sickness whenever he heard the word "stout." Worthington stout was his favorite beer. We've seen that dog more soused than his sappy boss Patrick.

Speaking of traveling salesmen, we've brought quite a few to their knees. If one of these stragglers sits down by the window with his imitation leather suitcase, it can be a while before anyone even gives him the time of day. Mostly he'll just sit there staring at the stubble-jawed, red-eyed regulars who've been playing at rami-whist since the day before. If he's brave enough to defy the silence he'll call out for a cup of coffee. Then Liza, Patrick's mother, will shout from behind the bar that the pub is closed.

"But the door was open! The lights are on!"

"Hard of hearing, sir? We're *closed*."

"And those fellows over there?" (Tilting his clean-shaven chin toward the players.)

"That's a private meeting," says Liza. Or if the man, the stranger, the nonplayer, insists: "That's family, sir."

To which Felix the Cat will invariably add: "We're all related by marriage."

Usually the man will clear his throat and slink off. Sometimes they curse. Or slam the door behind them.

That morning the Unicorn was full by ten o'clock.

Actually, sir, we're not obliged to meet at the Unicorn. Truth is, we could go round to any number of other gambling establishments, if only for variety's sake. There's plenty of gaming houses in our town as are tolerated and protected by the police. But we choose not to. Because it's only in the Unicorn that we feel at home.

Can you honestly picture us in the Parthenon, a few streets down? With all that pink plush, those candelabras left over from the Battle of the Golden Spurs, those Leatherette sofas that fart when you sit on 'em, with that palsy-walsy publican from Limburg wearing your ears off with his stale jokes! And that music they've got on the whole time. Music, when you're playing cards! Lord, no, we wouldn't be caught dead there.

The Unicorn is bigger than a breadbox, but only just, it stinks from the cesspit in the courtyard, the walls are hung with faded ads for beer that hasn't been brewed in a dog's age, from the days when every village had its own brewery, and there's usually a peevish Patrick behind the bar chewing on a cigar, but has anyone ever heard Patrick tell a joke? Or even seen him laugh? At the most a crooked grin, like he's champing on the lemon peel he always used to put in Rickabone's coffee.

It's three months now since Rickabone threw in his hand. Three months that he, as Frans the Dutchman says, can no longer hear the cock crow.

Passed away just in time, too, old Rickabone. All played out, he was. But we'll not go into that for the moment, it'd spoil our coffee and that'd be a damn shame seeing as how Patrick makes a stiff pot. With no chicory.

Rickabone always required a twist of lemon in his espresso, it was a habit he'd picked up in Italy. Ah well, to each his own.

Anyway, around half past ten Verbist the Schoolmaster walks in. Hasn't even got a pint in his hand and already he's shooting off at the mouth. By the way, you mustn't think for a minute, sir, that Verbist, that red-bearded, nearsighted, coddled egghead in jeans, is charged with the educational welfare of our innocent children, no, not even our town council, which drops one brick after another, is *that* stupid. No, we call Verbist a schoolmaster because he gives drawing lessons an hour or two a week at the Academy and because he sometimes forgets himself and starts preaching at us like we were in his class. About Unification and Relevance. And if it isn't Polyvalence, it's Deontology. He'll even venture a *Démasqué* every now and again. Sometimes he'll rail against his own craft and livelihood, because in his opinion the education of our children is a massacre, a conspiracy between Church and State and Education to keep us all firmly in line for the rest of our lives from the first day of school onward. Could be. But in the meantime that massacre is earning him three months' a year paid holiday.

3

So by half past ten Verbist is bringing out the big guns. His reddish beard, like the beard of some brute that's devoured his own children, wobbles up and down. "What we lack in this land are men of integrity! Great men! Men with spirit!"

Whereupon Felix the Cat sneers, "The greater the man, the greater the crap!"

Frans the Dutchman, who hates Felix the Cat, drawls, "And the smaller the dog, the bigger his yap."

Felix the Cat snarls, "A *Dutch* dog always returns to his vomit."

As you can see, spirits were flying in the Unicorn. It was gray outside. It was the middle of the week.

Then Verbist turns to Jake, one of the pillars of the Unicorn. We call him Jackie, Jocko, and occasionally, Jacob. He comes round every day, but if he loses more than a thousand francs he stops and looks on from his permanent spot beside the bar, next to the corridor, in the stink of ammonia, cauliflower, and cesspit.

"Day and night," says Verbist, "I'm not ashamed to say it, day and night I sit in my studio, struggling to paint someone who *isn't there.*"

"Why even try!" says Jake in the little voice that sounds so surprisingly high and thin for his two hundred and fifty pounds.

We love Jake. He may not have invented the light bulb, but he's got a heart like honeycake. We don't much like playing with him, though. He's too slow. Rickabone always used to say, "Jake, you've got to count your cards!" But Jake has a hard enough time remembering which is which.

It was Rickabone who first brought Jake to the Unicorn, and who once told us that Jake's name was really Jacob. "Jacob van Artevelde!" shouted some joker. "That's what it says on my birthday certification," came Jake's apologetic soprano.

When you think about it, Jake really is a bit like Jacob van

Artevelde, whose statue quiets the crowds in our market square with its raised bronze arm, and who believed in justice and fairness and for that reason got his head busted in Thirteen Hundred Such-and-Such. Because whenever there's a wrangle or a brawl at the Unicorn Jake always comes over, all two hundred and fifty pounds of him, and all he has to say is "Hey, hey, lads, are we through?" and they're through. Or nearly.

How Jake ended up at the Unicorn? Here's what happened. It was in the Early Days of Rickabone, in the Limbo before that glorious Hell that was to last for seventeen months, the Kingdom of Rickabone. At that time Rickabone didn't have a pot to piss in. Every day of the week he'd be in here badgering us. "Come now, surely you can spare a thousand francs? Not even five hundred?" And we'd keep on shelling it out. Naturally. Because who knew what was in store for Rickabone when his Pa and Ma kicked off? Untold wealth. His Ma was twice as rich as his Pa, and that man owned land, sir, as far as the eye could see.

Now, Pa Bone had said: "Rick, you're a first-class layabout, that's your own business, seems it's all the fashion nowadays among the young folks, but if you think, snot-nosed spawn of my ballocks, that you'll ever see one bloody franc of mine while I'm still alive, unless you get yourself a job . . ."

That's why Rickabone became a traveling salesman, or should we say, out of respect for the dearly departed: a sales representative. In Bics. Or as he called them, "ball pens." We Unicorners nearly split our sides when we heard that. *Ball* pens! But you know how it is, sir, players are just like kids. They don't give a damn what it is, so long as it's dirty.

One day, a day like any other, Rickabone's sitting at his usual table playing king, with Fernand and Tino I believe, and he's sipping his twelfth espresso-and-lemon, when in comes this beefy goliath in a light gray dustcoat who walks up behind him and stands there waiting, fat as bacon.

"What is it, Jake?" asks Rickabone, not taking his eyes off the cards for a second.

"You need to sign this, Mister Bone," says Tarzan, and that was the first time we ever heard that convent-school-girl voice of his.

"Just a moment, Jake." Rickabone goes on playing, and loses, of course. Because in the Early Days, we never let him win.

"Damn!" cries Rickabone. "How's a person supposed to concentrate!" He flings his cards down on the rug, which has an ad woven into it for some beer that no longer exists and was named after Peter Benoit, the musician from Harelbeke. Good beer, dark, a bit sweet.

"Jake, you numbskull, what do you want?" barks Rickabone. Jake hands him a piece of paper. Rickabone looks at it for a long time, sighs deeply, belches. "Sit down, Jake, and have a drink."

Jake has a Stella Artois.

"Where're the goods?"

"In my truck," says Jake. "Right outside."

On orders from Rickabone Jake hauls in the merchandise: ten thousand Bic pens packed in cardboard boxes. Rickabone grabs a fistful, holds them up in the air, and says: "Who will give me two thousand francs for a thousand of these magnificent, brand-new, international pens?"

Verbist tries out a few, drawing squiggles and lines all over a coaster, and then buys three thousand. Deontology or not, two francs for a pen that costs twenty at the Grand Bazar, now that's a bargain! But of course, you've got to have the Academy students to fob 'em off on.

"Anyone else?" cries Rickabone. Within minutes the whole load was sold. "You see," says Rickabone, "that's how easy it is to do business." He then went on to lose all that easily earned money in a couple of games of pontoon, slurping one espresso after another and swallowing handfuls of pink pills to calm his nerves.

That's how Jake found his way to the Unicorn, first in Rickabone's wake, and after that on his own, in all his shy, lonesome, solitary blubber.

He was good to his fellow man, our Jake. It was he, for instance, who used to wake up Pete the Milkman every morning in the back room of the Unicorn, six-thirty on the dot. "Come on, Pete, out you go, time for your rounds!" In order to do this Jake himself had to get up at six, even though he didn't have to be down at the warehouse till eight.

Speaking of which, there's another one that popped off before his time, Pete the Milkman. But what d'you expect, sir? His first milk round at half past seven, fresh bread round at ten o'clock sharp, quick game of whist, then checking tickets from two to eight at the Cinema Royal and back to the cards till three in the morning. Carry on like that and you're just asking for a pair of pine pajamas.

But he had fun, Pete the Milkman, that he did. And no end of affection. Specially from us clowns down at the Unicorn.

Is there anyone, for that matter, who isn't a welcome guest at the Unicorn? We get each other's backs up now and then, and there are one or two we wouldn't mind slicing to ribbons in a dark alley, but still, we're always glad to see each other. You've got to be a real bastard for us to turn you away from our tables. Now, I'm only talking about the regulars, of course. Anyone who walks in here unannounced, who we don't know, can expect our absolute, unconditional contempt. If you don't play, you don't exist.

Right. You wanted to hear about that morning? How it all began? Well, it was just past eleven, still not much action at the tables. Patrick's wife Marta was going around with chorizo, this Spanish stuff that burns holes in your tongue and you need three or four pints to recover. Old publican's trick. Jake, now that Verbist had finally quit bothering him, seemed to want to leave. Every now and again he said, "Ho-hum!"

Markie was there, a lad who's been through a lot in the course of his life, and Doctor Verbraeken, who's helping Markie forget what he's been through with pills that would knock out a hippo.

Deaf Derek, Staf van't Peperstraatje, and Frans the Dutchman were there. And oh yes, I've nearly left out the most important of all—Michel was there too.

Okay. This girl walks in, a blonde, seventeen years old, wearing a miniskirt. Well now. She says the mini is coming back in fashion. We're glad to hear it.

We look her up and down and then peek out from behind our cards at Gerald the Prick, who, ever since our sainted Rickabone passed away, has been our expert on tender young womenfolk. Gerald sticks out his lower lip and sucks in like you would on a hollow tooth, which means: "Not bad, she might do for Fernand, or even Verbist, but not for me in any case, nor for any other connoisseurs of my distinction." I should tell you, Gerald the Prick is hard to please. Never satisfied. Either the hips are too wide, or the thighs too round, or the ass too bony. Always something. Remember all the misery he caused us after he'd discovered that the one girl who'd finally charmed him had *ingrown nipples!* Three days of drivel about those nipples. A nightmare. But this blond mare, this daydream, she's a filly of a different color. We stare. Discreetly, of course. What's she doing here in our monastery, where you rarely ever see a woman, except maybe now and then a couple of wives of players who're making the rounds together.

The cards lie motionless in our hands. The whole Unicorn, even Verbist, is struck dumb.

She looks a bit like Brigitte Bardot. (Who you never hear much about these days, come to think of it. Wasn't she saving whales or something?) Brigitte Bardot, but then a younger version, with a lot less class.

She walks straight up to Felix the Cat, who's sitting there with a flush or a full house, you can tell by the so-called casual way he's stroking his prissy little moustache. She lays her hand on his Prince-of-Wales shoulder, that snakeskin, that pearl, that star in our silent stable of Bethlehem. "Mister Felix," she says, "you're a fine one!"

"How's that, Marianneke?" asks Felix the Cat, and sure enough, he lays a full house on the table and sweeps up the pot.

"I go all the way down to your salon for a water wave, specially, and you're not there!"

"But Marianneke, you know you're supposed to call first and make an appointment."

"Do I?" she says. She sits down, smoothes her mini, raises a knee, and sticks her pink, stiletto-heeled sandal between the rungs of Felix's chair, so that, your attention please, gentlemen of the card table, her mussel has *got* to be open. Most of the players are praying they'll turn into cockroaches so they can scuttle under her chair and gaze right up at the fruit of paradise. Or perhaps cockroaches don't have eyes. Do they? We'll have to ask Doctor Verbraeken sometime.

"You told me yourself, Mister Felix, that I should come whenever I felt the need," says Marianneke.

Felix the Cat turns to her with his pearliest smile, his moistest lips, his burning-est eyes. "And do you feel the need right now, my dear?"

"Come on, Felix. Deal. It's your turn," says Markie impatiently.

Markie isn't one for the women. That's often the case with sportsmen who take too many pills.

"Quiet," snaps Felix the Cat. He deals quickly. We ante up. No big stakes. It's too early. Not the right weather for it either. Hard to play with that slut in the way.

Felix the Cat looks over his shoulder and says: "Marianneke, my sweet, go down to the salon and ask Liliane . . ."

"Oh, no!" she says. "You know I can't stand Liliane touching my hair."

"Well then, sweetness, have a martini and I might just go with you. And I promise," adds Felix the Tiger, casting a triumphant glance around the Unicorn, "I'll give you the full treatment."

"I don't want a martini," she says.

"What *do* you want?"

"Nothin'. How much longer's this game going to last?"

"Now, now, hold on," says Felix. "You mustn't rush me." And right before our blinded eyes, right beneath our snuffling noses, she changes, that mermaid Marianne, into a nag, a ball-breaker, a meddling spouse. Felix the Cat is so miffed by this metamorphosis that he takes an exceptionally long time pondering his cards. We suspect he's holding a flush.

Mademoiselle Marianne is offended, it seems. She searches the room and spots Michel in his corner. He looks the other way, right into the boil on Markie's neck. You're bound to get things like that with all those chemicals in your blood. Not even Doctor Verbraeken can do anything to prevent it.

Michel has long, curly eyelashes. Too long for a man.

"Hey," says Marianne. "Who do we have here! Michel."

"In the flesh," says Michel.

"How're you?"

"And you?"

"Could be worse," she says. She slides off her chair (the seat of which, if you can believe all those dirty books, must be sopping by now) and sashays over to the telephone, shoves the helplessly grinning Jake aside by the elbow, picks up the receiver, and starts gabbing to her fiancé.

She giggles, wriggles, shrieks, sways, and moans under the radar of our discreet glances. Ten minutes of laughter, neighing, astonished cries. "No! You're not *serious!* You do? Ha ha! Really? *My God . . .*"

Now what's our sly friend Staf up to, sitting there at the dice board? In the heat of the game (did you see me wink, sir?) he drops a die and it falls—isn't life strange!—right at the feet of the telephoning temptress. She bends her knees slightly and sticks out her ass, only the telephone wire's too short, she can't reach the die, but no matter, because Staf is already down on his knees looking for it, even though there's nothing to look for, the die is right in front of his nose, a six, but Staf grovels around on the floor just the same, bright red, from nerves or excitement (we can't tell which), and then looks up. Marianne carelessly slides her legs a bit farther apart. As she chatters on into the phone, which is half hidden in the straw-colored curtain of hair—"Why of *course*, Leon, of *course*. What? No. *Seriously?* You've got to be kidding . . ."—it dawns on us that Staf has a panoramic view of her Garden of Eden.

Invisible, inaudible applause accompanies Staf as he returns to his table. Deaf Derek stands him a beer and says thoughtfully, "Well, well, you old rascal, you!"

We're already rubbing our hands with glee because we know Derek, he won't rest until he's disparaged Staf's reckless deed, done him one better.

Without so much as a knowing wink at any of us, Derek steps up to Jake at the bar and starts calling him names. Every name in the book, sir. Why? To impress that mini-goddess on the phone? No, it's merely a trick, a stratagem worthy of the Unicorn, but Jake doesn't realize this, of course, his eyes and ears are full of clay. Derek puts on the screws, dragging Jake's wife down in his flood of abuse.

"Whuh?" says Jake, stunned. "My wife, a slut? Is that you, Derek, saying a thing like that . . ."

"Yes," says Deaf Derek. "And right to your face, too. Right smack between the eyes, right under your *horns.*"

"You, you, goddamn . . ." roars Jake, and, as was to be expected, the fuming rhino that lies trapped and smothered in Jake's opulent flesh breaks free. He grabs Derek, who's still smirking, by the loins and lifts him up until that grinning, graying head nearly touches the ceiling. Just when Jake is about to crack him like a nut, Derek leans over and hisses frantically into his hackles: "Not so hard, birdbrain, it's just pretend. *Pretend,* you idiot!"

"Oh," says Jake, and loosens his grip.

"Fall down," whispers Derek.

"Why?" asks Jake.

"That's why, stupid."

"But Derek . . ." The colossus is bewildered.

"So you can see her knickers," Derek urges in secret, shameless whispers that we can only guess at, because we're filling in this lecherous lisping, have no fears about that, sir, with our own, unspoken prayers.

"Oh, her *knickers,*" says Jake much too loudly, and for a moment we're afraid Marianne'll hear it, but she rattles on, in modulated discords, to her chéri. She's enjoying the fight, for naturally she assumes that it's because of her doe's eyes and BeeBee pout that these rams are battering each other, and she expects to see this card-game emporium transformed into an altar where men sing vespers to her inviolable beauty in the raucous stammering of Jake and Derek and where the priests, for want of her lubricated ribs, embrace each other.

To cut a long story short, the two go rolling around on the floor, right past her, arms and elbows flailing against her heavenly knees.

"Oooh, oooh!" squeals Venus. And prattles enthusiastically into the horn that all hell's broke loose down at the Unicorn.

Meanwhile the other players are collecting trumps and guessing at the trumps in each other's paws and acting like the fight is no more than a bit of clownish diversion amid the icy passion of the card game. Then all of a sudden the show's over and Derek gets up off the floor. He's not smiling anymore. No, there's something demure, diffident, on his ruddy horsebreeder's face—how shall I put it? We all see that Deaf Derek's face, usually so jauntily, indefatigably mirthful, now looks *serious*.

Jake looks serious too, but then he always does, even when he's laughing. Now that I'm on the subject, Jake only ever really laughs *along*, with other people, that is. Never of his own accord.

The two warriors beat the dust out of their clothes. Marianne has gone off to powder her nose. "Well? Well? Well?" we ask in hushed voices as Derek sits down to catch his breath.

Dully, as if he's saying, "Pass," he says: "She's got no knickers on."

"Come off it!" we say.

"She's got *black* knickers on," says a quick thinker.

13

Derek nods. "Black, yes, but it was 'r own hair."

"Quit fooling!"

"Or p'rhaps it was a thatch of flies," says Derek.

A while later, after a cognac or three, he says: "If it *was* knickers, they were awful small. And all wedged up . . . you know."

"What color?"

"Bit on the purply side."

"Ahh, hmm," we give this some thought.

"You ought to be ashamed," growls Doctor Verbraeken. "Grown men like yourselves . . ." But we pay no attention to him. Or to Verbist, who says something scornful to the effect of "hygenic function of *idées fixes* in the intoxication of the soul." Or to the yapping of Hairmaster Felix the Cat, who simply can't wait to drag his client, his young protégée, under the drier. That's plain as a pikestaff.

And sure enough, when Marianne returns, Felix the Cat wastes no time talking to her, in his most fatherly tone of voice, promising to take her in hand himself, personally, this very instant, down at Salon Felix.

Marianne trips behind his Prince-of-Wales arse to the door, but only after fixing Michel with an astonishingly soulless gaze. We all saw it, sir.

That's when the interrogation hits the fan.

"Was the hair inky-black or did it have a browny sheen?"

"Was it curly hair, or more like a rug?"

"Did she have, you know, a bump, or was it flat?"

"Were her knickers, that's assuming there *was* knickers, see-through? With those fancy holes in 'em? And little curls poking through?"

"Was it wet, or what?"

The accused, Jake and Derek, stand there looking sheepish.

Jake claims he didn't see a thing because he was too busy fighting off that hothead.

"Nothing at all?" we cry in dismay.

"Well, uh, p'rhaps a bit of shadow."

Staf van't Peperstraatje speaks for us all when he says: "Jake, Jake, Jake, the pair that made you must've had their eyes crossed!"

That's when (and opinions may differ on this, as they so often do concerning our national history), that's when Frans the Dutchman picked a fight with Michel. Frans is from Holland, a Dutchman, which is to say: a busybody and a know-it-all. He doesn't bat an eyelid when he says that Holland is the conscience of the world. In business affairs, too, he's every inch the Dutchman, which is to say, if he hasn't cheated you it's only because he's forgotten. Apart from that he's polite to the ladies, he whines a bit when he loses at cards, but not half as much as Staf or Deaf Derek, to name only two, and for the rest he's hyper-super-sensitive. He'll start bawling over absolutely nothing. It seems that when Frans goes to the movies and the little lost dog or the snot-nose everyone gave up for missing turns up again to the sound of a thousand violins, he blubbers like a widow that's lost her pension.

Okay. Now Markie is stupid enough to say what a damn shame it is that Rickabone couldn't be here to see this, *this* being the memorable pastorale of the Straddle-legged Marianne and her Two Tussling Voyeurs. And Frans the Dutchman, who, knowing himself too well, didn't even have the nerve to go to Rickabone's funeral (he'd probably have ended up jumping right into the grave along with the coffin or, worse still, falling into the arms of Rickabone's millionaire mother), Frans shakes his head, his eyeballs go double and pink and wet and he says: "Rickabone, oh, Rickabone, never again will you hear the cock crow . . ."

To which Michel yells: "For Christ's sake, when's it going to end, all that whining and nagging and moaning about Rickabone!"

Now Michel doesn't usually fly off the handle like that, on the contrary, he's always quite restrained, Michel is, like he's got something up his sleeve. We're surprised, especially when he adds: "Besides, he's probably all rotted away by now, old Rickabone, right down to the bone."

That does it. Frans starts ragging Michel, in earnest—and in Dutch. Verbist butts in too, spouting a string of maxims and sayings in his highbrow Flemish like he's standing in front of his class. He claims, among other things, that the trouble with Michel, like that of all young people nowadays who have been spoiled and stupefied and who no longer have any respect and no re-cep-*tiv-i-ty* and, eh, what was it he said about Michel's troubles? I can't think of it just now, but something was wrong in any case, says Verbist, and he comes to the conclusion that Michel is suffering from *anhedonia*.

"What's that?" asks an inquisitive player. Verbist shrugs. Doctor Verbraeken says that, according to him, although he could be wrong, of course, it means: an incapacity for experiencing pleasure.

"You mean, he's got no lead in his pencil?"

"No," says the Doctor. "It's more of a mental thing. Can't feel pleasure, can't feel grief."

Then Jake says, and he seems to be apologizing for stepping in: "Hey, hey, lads, are we through?"

"Ah, Rickabone, poor Rickabone," says Frans the Dutchman softly.

"It's not respectful," says Jake, "Michel bringing up the condition of our friend Rickabone's flesh just now. But then," he adds tonelessly, "life is life."

"There's no spirit here, in this land, no spirit, that's the whole point!" cries the schoolteacher.

"Did Rickabone have spirit?" asks Michel. "Did he? No! Not an ounce of spirit in his whole body, in that whole damn bag of Rickabones!"

Well, that certainly goes down the wrong way. A chorus of protests rises from all sides. The dice fall silent.

"Jake," says Michel, "you've followed Rickabone into nearly every casino in Europe, from here to Finland. You tell me, did he have one drop of spirit in his whole damn body?"

"He was my pal," says Jake.

"Mine too!" shouts Michel. "But that's not the question!"

"He had no less spirit than anybody else," snorts Frans the Dutchman.

"Jake, I want to know your opinion, yours alone," Michel demands.

Jake starts picking his nose. "Spirit, hmm . . . ," he says, wiping his finger on his apron.

"Did he have it, or didn't he?"

"No."

"There!" says Michel. "Finally you get to hear it from somebody else."

"Michel," says Deaf Derek, "you are not worthy, sir, of our leastmost attention."

"That's right," says the Dutchman.

"Just tell me straight out, I'm not wanted here!" says Michel.

"Yes. That's right," says the Dutchman.

"You heard it yourself," says Deaf Derek.

"Loud and clear," says Michel, his voice suddenly quiet. When he gets up we notice, as we so often do, how very deceptively some people can be put together. When he's sitting at the table holding his cards and scratching himself, Michel looks normal enough, but the moment he gets up and walks across the black and white squares of linoleum to the door, that's when you see how short his legs really are. The Germans call someone like that a *Sitzriese*. Although the Germans would've shot him on sight during the war, with that nose, and that mess of curls on his pate. His great-grandfather was Portuguese, says Michel. I don't believe it for a minute. He's one of *them* and he can't hide it. On the other hand, he also has a touch of the Moor in him. With that yellowish skin and those fat lips. Let's just say, Michel is not one of us.

"Hey, hey, lads," says Jake.

"Save your breath, Jake," says Michel, "I get the message. Rickabone's turned into a damn saint around here, a martyr. Fine with me, but don't expect me to sing a mass for him."

He goes to the front door and stands in the sunlight that pours through the curtains.

"So long, folks, and to hell with you all," says Michel.

"You haven't settled up yet—" says Patrick the Boss.

"That's your problem," says Michel. "You've made enough money off of me as it is." But he can't mean what he says, it sounds too defiant, too fierce. Patrick chews his cigar.

"And as for the rest of you losers," says Michel, his hand on the doorknob, "I've had it up to here with all of you. The school-teacher's right, there's no spirit in this land. I'm sure glad I won't have to be seeing your ugly mugs for a while. Because, gentlemen, I'm off to America."

Frans the Dutchman bleats, Staf yawns, Deaf Derek looks incredulous, the doctor grins. Outside is a traffic jam, dozens of cars honk their horns, an ambulance arrives on the scene.

Michel says we're all a miserable bunch of piddlers, because a serious player plays for serious money and that only happens in the U.S. of A.

Which is a load of hogwash, of course. Because ever since the day the Unicorn first opened its doors there's been many a fortune gone up in smoke. We cleaned out a flax merchant in less than three weeks, Poelinckx the Contractor had to sell off sixteen houses, and didn't our hero, our saint, Rickabone, our household god, blow twelve million Belgian francs in eleven months?

That's why we pay no attention to the yapping of that half-breed. And our flagrant disdain tickles his chromosomes. He's trembling, Michel is.

"Jake," says he.

"Yes, Michel?"

"These jerks have been making a fool out of you long enough. You've got more spirit in your little finger than all of them put together. You're my buddy, Jake, you and nobody else. And that's why I'm inviting you, where everyone can hear, to come along with me to America. I'll pay your fare personally, out of my own pocket."

The buzzing of a blowfly. The rustling of the doctor's newspaper. Markie's dry cough. The murmuring tap. A chair scraping the floor.

"By boat?" asks Jake.

"By plane. Charter flight."

"Me?"

"Yes, you."

"Where to?"

"Across the ocean. There and back. To Las Vegas, where the real players are. Twelve days. Is it yes or no?"

"It's yes," says Jake. "A hundred an' fifty procent."

In the hallowed silence that follows, Markie says, "Well kiss my ass."

And so it happened that the first seed was sown and the idea of the journey took root, and that those two, Michel, the accused, and Jake, the innocent, set their course for where the pineapples, neon lights, and green dollars grow, and I'll have to confess, sir, that we at the Unicorn were struck with awe.

2

CURSING, MICHEL DUG AROUND in the fashionably slanted, too goddamn narrow pockets of his aubergine-leather jacket, but he couldn't find his keys. They must've been lying somewhere under a bench in the Unicorn, in the dust and grit, among cigarette butts and beer coasters with the scores of last week's king game jotted down in ballpoint. As he stood there waiting, his finger on the bell, he imagined Staf van 't Peperstraatje finding the keys and slipping them into his pocket and then, that afternoon, when Mama was asleep and he, Michel, was standing in line at the unemployment office, Staf breaking into the house and discovering, in the little room upstairs, under the bed, the *Hitlerjugend* knife and the airgun and the weepy love letters from Markie, and how Staf would smirk at the sight of his enemy's stash, these secret, precious possessions, and flee the house, quickly, and head for the Unicorn, where he'd whisper to his brothers in arms: "Just like Rickabone. Yes. Seen it with me own eyes. Even a gun. Knife, too. Just like our dear departed Rickabone."

Michel heard his mother's shuffling footsteps. She opened the door and smiled at him with a slow nod of her grizzled head. Her lioness's head. Clutching the doorjamb with white, chapped claws, she stepped aside to let him pass. Her quilted robe fell open; he looked away from the bony frame in the blue-flowered nightgown. She was in pain. She smiled at him. She was glad he had come.

"Thought you'd never get here," she said, almost cheerfully, and patted his hip. "We're having codfish and cauliflower."

"No butter sauce," he said.

She kept smiling, with grayish, even teeth, with dry lips, his lips.

"You look so angry. Did you lose much?"

"No," he said, and knew he looked sullen, and that she was remembering his father, his real father, whom he resembled at moments like these. (Jan, his other father, would soon be home from work.) Michel's mother had often remarked to him that his father looked unhappy, for no apparent reason, it was the shape of his face, she said, the bones perhaps, and she found it hard to take, especially early in the morning when he'd be sitting there at breakfast looking like the sky had caved in.

The whole kitchen smelled of her, of dead flowers.

"Are you sure you won't have any sauce?"

"No."

"It's not as good without—"

"You heard me," said Michel. She began rummaging around in the cupboard under the sink.

"Your stomach acting up again?"

"Yes."

Gin didn't agree with Michel, and he had drunk five glasses down at the Unicorn. (So as not to be outdone by the rest. Some day, very soon, I'll do whatever I want wherever I want. I'll stroll right into the Unicorn and order chocolate milk.)

"Why are you smiling?"

He decided to be nice to her.

22

"I won today, at the Unicorn."

"How much?"

"Four thousand francs." She growled, then muttered something at the refrigerator. He noticed that the hair on her crown had thinned and resolved to say nothing about his trip to America until the very last minute. Phone her from the airport. Or send a telegram from Los Angeles. He wished she would hurry up with the codfish, and hoped that the sickly smell would mask her own.

The walls of the kitchen were papered with fanciful sprigs of exotic flowers, but the paper had been sloppily hung and you could see the dark gray cement between the strips. Jan, his other father, had done the job.

On the plastic tablecloth lay *Het Volk*, the crossword puzzle half done, and two bloodstained handkerchiefs.

Michel was tempted to go straight up to his room and switch on BRT 2, or read another chapter from *Rommel, the Desert Fox*, or practice with his dagger in front of the mirror. But he was feeling strangely generous tonight.

(She hasn't got much longer to live, and I'm her greatest . . . what am I saying? Her only joy. I'll wait until I've got her propped up safe and sound on the parlor sofa, in front of the TV. Soften the blow. It'll have to be tonight.)

He was immediately seized by a fierce, almost mournful feeling of sadness. He hadn't come away from the Unicorn unscathed, goddamit, he had let himself be carried away by a childish need to prove himself to those bastards. (Did you really think you'd floored 'em, bowled 'em over, inviting that moron Jake along? And where the hell are you going to get the money?)

His mother cleaned the fish and whined about Jan, his other father. Her voice grew slightly agitated, as it always did when she talked about him.

"He just better not think I'll be sitting here in the kitchen waiting for him to come home. He can heat up his own codfish. 'Cause soon as we're through eating I'm going straight into that parlor and sit down on the sofa and give my feet a rest. That's right. I've had my hands full with him again, you can't imagine. 'Cause here it is end of the month and he's clear out of drinking money."

Her dry mouth gasped for breath.

After supper they played dominoes in the parlor. He let her win, but for the first time he had the feeling she didn't even care who won. (She's dying.)

He wished she were dead. Then there would be a neat, precise, calculable period of grief, and then a memory that would fade, disappear. Now the cancer was eating her up, slowly, daily, painfully, right before his eyes. Now he had to sit by and watch, acting out these sanctimonious charades just to make her happy. Mama, Mama.

He wondered whether she would still be alive when he returned from his trip. To his surprise and dismay, he suddenly felt his eyes stinging. "Should we watch 'Luck of the Draw'?" he asked.

"If you like."

She looked more at him than at the TV.

"I wish I could get away for a while," he said. "Ten days or so."

"It'd be good for you," she said.

"Maybe I'll do it, too," he said. His mother fixed her eyes on the contestants, who were prancing about on a twirling cylinder, dressed as minstrels, while their opponents sprayed them with fire hoses. (I'm dancing, too, Mama, even wilder, even crazier. Your death, Mama, the luck of the draw.)

"Ten days?" she asked.

24

"Sure. Something like that."

She eased herself up off the sofa and got two beers, lit a ciga-rette, and handed it to him.

"When was Doctor Verbraeken here last?" asked Michel.

"Why?"

"No reason."

"Got to be at least fourteen days ago," she said crossly.

"I'll ask him to stop by."

"You don't have to."

"Yes I do."

"I can manage fine on my own," said Michel's mother. "You go on vacation, don't worry about me."

"Maybe, I said."

She turned her broad, gray, leonine face to him. She smiled, in triumph and despair. When Jan came home and filled the parlor with his innocent, exuberant stories, Michel, without a word to him, went up to his room. He stood in front of the closet mirror stripped to the waist and lunged twelve times, kicked seven, but it was pathetic. Suddenly he saw, just above his shoulder, crouched in a corner of the mirror and looking perfectly relaxed, the dear departed Rickabone. When Rickabone felt Michel's gaze he arched his thin, flawless brows, tossed a lavender pill in the air, and caught it on his tongue. He mumbled something, but Michel could hear it clear as glass, for he had heard him say it so many times before: "An honest man never wins."

Michel punched out helplessly at Rickabone's Adam's apple, with clenched fist, with outstretched fingers, with the palm of his hand.

3

DIDI IS HUMMING AS SHE DRAWS, something by the Beatles. In the old days, when she was well, Jake would often sing the melody along with her, sometimes even the refrain. When Didi recited her English lessons, Jake could understand her perfectly. In the old days.

Didi has outlined the figures with a black felt-tip pen: Suske, Wiske, and Aunt Sidonia, just like in her comic book. Now she's busily filling in Wiske's hair with four or five different colored pencils. She licks her lips, again and again.

"Is Wiske off to the Carnival, with all those colors in her hair?"

"She's not going anywhere," says Didi. "She's staying right here on paper."

Sometimes Didi calls her father Suske. "Silly Suske, stupid Suske." But never when Dina's around, as if she knows that it isn't really true, that Jake doesn't look at all like Suske, that Jake is Papa and Dina, Mama. Jake is careful never to call her Wiske. Though sometimes he'd like to, whenever she calls him Suske. But the curate has cautioned him. "Whatever happens, you must never encourage her in these delusions."

When Dina comes in, the first thing she does is open the window. Jake stubs out his cigar. Didi doesn't look up, just goes on coloring. You can see her tongue.

Dina flops down onto a chair, her yellow plastic straw bag clasped between her knees. Jake is frightened. Something has happened, he can tell by the look in her eyes.

Didi stops humming. Sidonia's hair is all done, too: sea green, purple, and orange.

"How were things at the Unicorn?" asks Dina.

"Quiet. I didn't stay long, half an hour maybe."

Dina scratches the shiny straw with her long, narrow index finger. In the old days Jake used to know what size shoes Dina wore. Now he'd have to guess. She wiggles the pointy black shoe up and down.

"Didi, have you been at the peanut butter again?"

"Nope," answers Didi, indifferent. Only now does Jake notice the dried, brownish blob in the corner of his daughter's mouth, like a wart. He takes Didi's face in his hands and picks it off. She lets him, her eyes still on the drawing.

Dina's eyes, cat's eyes, gleam cold and gray in the darkened room. Jake picks up the ashtray and tips the remains of his cigar into the toilet bowl. When he comes back Dina says to her daughter: "You're as big a liar as your father. Go in the other room."

"I still got to color in Aunt Sidonia's apron."

"Didi, you know what happens to little girls who tell lies. Now march straight into the other room, or else."

Didi does as she's told and walks slowly out the door. Moments later Jake hears her in the front room, reeling off Hail Marys in a high, fervent voice.

"Has she eaten?"

"French fries. A whole bagful."

"Anything else?"

"Mixed pickles," says Jake. He bought her a garlic sausage, too, but Didi threw it at a man on a bike. She used to be crazy about garlic sausage. Now she's down on her knees in front of a photo of Saint Thérèse of Lisieux. Her prayer slows. How many Hail Marys were there again for lying? The curate has said that what matters most is the rhythm, the hypnotic effect.

"I hope you're satisfied," says Dina. "All the girls at Salon Felix were laughing at me. Your old pal Felix, too. Thought I didn't notice. But it'll take a lot more than that to make a fool out of me."

"Felix, too?"

"Him most of all."

"Oh?" So that's what happened.

"I'll survive, I won't let it get me down, but I can think of better ways to spend an afternoon."

"I can imagine," says Jake.

"Aren't you even going to ask why they were having such a high old time?"

"Why?"

Dina screams, without making a sound. Sometimes everything in Dina, including her voice, stops dead, as if her whole body is locked in an aluminum corset, the bony face with the layer of pancake, the scarlet lips, the choked howling.

"Don't you think you might've told me? Even if you knew I'd be against it? Does the whole town have to know before I do? So they can laugh in my face while I stand there blinking like a moron?"

The curate told her she should never use that word, not even think it.

"Moron?"

"I'm not talking about Didi, I'm talking about me." But her rage has been sidetracked. She stands up. "America," she says. "Why not the North Pole?"

"We'll be passing through," says Jake.

"What?"

"We're flying *over* the North Pole," he says. "If all goes well."

After reciting her penance Didi wanders up to her room and starts playing a Beatles song on the piano.

"I wanted to tell you, Dina, honest, but Michel said it was better not to let folks know till everything was arranged, the tickets, the reservations . . ."

She pulls off her coat, flings it over a chair, which is very unlike her, sits back down, whips one elegant leg over the other.

("Dina's a thoroughbred," Staf van't Peperstraatje once said. "Ever seen them ankles?")

"So when were you planning on leaving, you coward?" she asks dully.

"Beginning of next week."

"Well, you can just forget the whole idea," she says in the same tone. Her foot is jiggling again.

"I already arranged everything at work, the foreman says it's okay. Leon'll stand in for me."

Dina brings the oval wristwatch, the one she inherited from her mother, right up to her face. Her movements are suddenly brusquer, though restrained. She parts her knees, clasps her bag between them, reaches into the bag, takes out a compact, and touches up her lipstick. Then she leans way back and squeezes blue drops in her eyes, the kind you're only allowed to use once a month, or you'll get cataracts.

"Ow," she says. Blue dye runs down her cheeks. "Ow." Her eyes squeezed shut, her mouth contorted with pain, Dina gropes around in her bag until she finds a Kleenex. She dabs her eyelids. For the rest of the evening the whites of her eyes will have a pale blue sheen.

Didi comes into the room and asks, "What's Mama playing?"

"Go upstairs," says Dina.

"I can't play piano anymore. My hands're all tired of playing," says Didi reproachfully. This reproach is aimed solely at Jake. Jake never tires of looking at Didi, she's more beautiful than any woman he knows. She can tear out his wispy hair, grind her heels into his belly, dance all over him, he wouldn't care.

"Then don't play," says Dina, glancing at her watch.

After a few scales from upstairs, followed by a long silence, Dina says: "And with Michel of all people! That maggot. Never done a stitch of work in his life and always up to no good. He'd skin you alive if he had the chance, that half a nigger—"

"Nigger? That's jumping to confusions. I mean, con*clu*sions."

"All right, he can't help it, that was his mother's fault, but he is and always will be a half a Turk or a Moroccan or whatever he is."

"His father was Portuguese."

"Yes, yes, we know all about that! And this is the scum you go off with, hand-in-hand, to the other side of the world!"

Half an hour too late, a half hour in which Dina crosses and uncrosses her legs a dozen times and sits up straighter than usual, the bell rings and Jake opens the door for the curate.

"Hello?" says the curate, as always, as if he's on the phone. This evening he's wearing a black leather jacket and a red-and-blue-checked lumberjack shirt. And as always, there's a hungry look on his pointed face, with its flaxen brows and lashes.

In the hallway Jake tells him, "Didi's said at least twenty Hail Marys this evening."

"Really?" exclaims the curate. "And what has she done wrong?"

"She told a lie," says Dina.

"Ah, yes," he says. Jake would like to wipe that pitying smile right off his face.

Jake disappears into the bathroom with the *Zondagskrant*. Now those two'll start talking about the unshakable faith everybody's supposed to have, about positive thinking, about transcendentalism. Jake had to repeat "transcendentalism" at least thirty times before it stuck. He'd have to try it out some afternoon in the Unicorn, on Verbist, he won't know what hit him! But the opportunity hasn't presented itself, not yet, because Jake isn't entirely sure what it means, that word, it's something that doesn't ordinarily happen to ordinary people leading ordinary lives, if they use their common sense, that is, no, it's something that takes place above and beyond our world, and that's why Dina has latched onto this boy scout of a priest who tosses around such words the way we'd say "ace of hearts" or "This round's on me, Patrick," and why shouldn't Dina lean on him? After all the grief she's had from doctors and psychiatrists, Doctor Verbraeken included, gnawing away at her and Didi like that dachsie in the Unicorn with his rubber bone! Why shouldn't she, if it'll ease the curse that came over Didi eight years back and left her with the brains of a chimpanzee, a child of six?

The curate nips at a glass of Elixir d'Anvers, a syrupy yellow drink that would make any ordinary person puke. Now if that isn't a sign of "transcendentalism"!

They're talking, as they often have lately, about a dream Dina's had.

Some mornings, before his fried eggs and bacon are on the table, Jake has to wait until Dina, hunched over in her peignoir, has finished scribbling down everything she has dreamed about the night before. Otherwise she'll have forgotten it all by the time the curate arrives. Jake has read several of these notes, while she was in the bathroom. On the back of a page torn off the calendar she had once written, in blue ballpoint, in her round hand: "Garden full of thorns. I sit there knitting like a maniac, faster and faster till I lose track of the stitches. Pain in my stomach too. Ask cur.: thorns?"

When Jake walks back in, the conversation flags. "Well, you certainly aren't losing any weight over it, are you, Jake?" says the priest jovially.

"He eats like there's no tomorrow," says Dina.

"It's nerves," says Jake, and is then furious because it sounds so apologetic. He sits down in his rattan armchair with the *Zondagskrant* and searches Dina's face for a trace of what he once saw when she came out of the confessional at St. Michael's. She was staggering, drooling, she could barely find her way back to her seat, but when he grabbed her arm to steady her she looked at him, her own husband, with such loathing and horror and amazement, you'd think it was he who had brought down the curse on Didi's head. That was in the first few weeks. When she kneeled on the cane seat in a haze of incense and candlewax, he stroked her bowed back, and she let him.

Jake doesn't see a trace.

They just can't resist, those two, they start gabbing about Dina's dream all over again. Exactly how it works, Jake's not sure, but the idea is that Dina tells everything that's bothering her, including her dreams, to the curate, who takes it all in, charges his batteries, you might say, and then discharges them on Didi, along with Indian chants and laying on of hands, while she kneels before the photo of Saint Thérèse of Lisieux.

"Didi loves it. It helps, it helps," says Jake very, very quietly behind his *Humo* magazine. "But how long does it have to go on, this circus, this hocus-pocus, before we can even begin to hope that Didi's engine'll start running again? I know, it helps, every little bit helps, and she is better, much better than in the first few months of the curse, when she attacked Dina, ripped open her blouse, and started clawing at Dina's breast and sucking at it like a starving baby, and she was sixteen years old."

Jake reads in the *Zondagskrant* about a colony of sea lions that are making their way down the Canadian coast, toward California. He's heading that way too. He laughs. He's been called a lot of names in his time, at work, in the army, in the Unicorn, "elephant," "hippo," even "whale." But "sea lion"? No, not yet.

Dina is speaking in a measured voice. It seems that last night's dream was about a desert in which she had lost her way because she was looking for something.

"What?" asks the curate tenderly.

"I don't know. I just kept digging around in the sand."

"Had you ever been in that desert before?"

"Never. It looked like one of those deserts in the movies, where the cowboys are always galloping after each other. California."

"Sorehead," says Jake.

"Come, come," says the curate.

"Jake's leaving me," says Dina. "He's flying away. Mr. Globetrotter here is jetting off to California."

"So I've heard," says the curate.

"What? Where?" screams Dina. Her aluminum corset cracks, bursts.

"These things get around."

Dina pours him another Elixir d'Anvers, buries her face in her bony hands.

"To be honest," says the curate, "though I wouldn't want to

interfere more than absolutely necessary, but I am, after all, responsible for your spiritual welfare, and Dina's, I really don't believe it would be a good idea, Jake, under the circumstances—"

"Did I offend you or something?" asks Jake.

"This has nothing to do with offense. I merely feel that you're allowing yourself to get carried away."

"By those lowlives down at the pub," says Dina from behind her hands.

"I truly understand, Jake, you need a bit of diversion from the daily grind, something to alleviate the sense of alienation that has set in after all these years of hard labor . . ." He stops. There's a loud, mechanical, drumming sound just above his head.

Didi is dancing.

"Didi!" Dina hollers at the ceiling. "Go to bed!" And without pausing for a breath she says urgently, "That woman was there again, at the entrance to the Grand Bazar, she's there every day of the week waiting for me to show up, she knows I do my shopping there, and she held out her hand to Didi again and said, 'What a pretty child.'"

The drumming above their heads has grown duller and slower, as if Didi has moved onto something soft. Jake can't bear to (and mustn't) think of his maimed little goddess feverishly trampling the faded Persian rug, a pillow pressed against her cheek.

The curate picks bits of lint off his new lumberjack shirt.

"Every time you come here, you start talking about *alienation*, and how I'm a victim of my work," says Jake. "What d' you know about my work? I've never seen you down at Herreman's."

"He sees more than you think," snarls Dina.

The curate rubs lightly over the drawing with all the colors of the rainbow, as if to see whether the colors will rub off.

"Didi is at a critical phase," he says, "and extremely vulnerable.

34

We're on the right track, there's hope in sight, but she's far from cured, and that is why I strongly urge you, Jake, to reconsider your plan, to think seriously about whether this is the time, and I'm thinking of Dina as well, whether this is the time to, how shall I put it, to abandon them."

He rubs harder at the wobbly, brightly colored figures in the drawing.

Jake bites the inside of his cheek, tastes blood. He looks away from the thin, tensed muscles in the priest's neck. The muffled dance above them goes on and on. Jake looks away from the priest's hands, the spatulate fingers with the chewed-off nails that hold up the Body of Christ, that caress the dead and perform last rites and are now stroking Didi's colors, and his heart is pounding, faster than the drumming above his head. He goes to the door. He flees from them both, leaving them to do what they please, all evening long, with his battered flesh and blood, Didi.

4

SEEING AS HOW WE AT THE UNICORN, and most players in fact, prefer to live our lives on the edge of things, and seeing as how we, as Verbist the Schoolmaster would say: escape from the totalitarian and egalitarian pressures of the system by retreating into the illusion of the game, you'd think we'd be sworn friends, or as Verbist would say: *united*.

Wrong, sir.

The plan was for the whole Unicorn to go along to the airport in a special bus and, after saying our farewells, drive straight up to the wharf in Ostend for fresh lobster, then a bar or two, then off to the Casino, where they wouldn't be able to get rid of us till we'd broken the bank. Nice thought. But you know how it goes. Words, words, words. Felix the Cat couldn't get away from the salon, Deaf Derek had to go down to the courthouse for disrespect to a public servant in the execution of his duties, or some such thing, Staf had to collect his brats from school because his wife's got galloping consumption, Verbist wanted to come, but then his sweetie, Olga, would have had to come too, and that was out of the question, because Olga always wants to get home before dark and the thought of listening to Olga moaning and groaning all night long—sorry, sir, but there are limits. Anyway, when all was said and done there were (hang onto your seat!) four of us. Jake, Michel, Rev'em-up Red, and me. In Rev'em-up Red's Jaguar, ninety miles an hour with one hand tied behind his back.

Some folks say he's called Red because when he gets angry his face turns red as a beet, others'll tell you it's because he's a communist (now, I'm not saying it was from the bottom of his heart but he did run on the communist party ticket during the elections, even if it was just to screw his dad the conservative councilman). And the "Rev'em-up" part, that's simple: he's mad about motorcycles. He's got six.

So, we're bowling down the highway. Jake, in back, is white as a sheet. His wife, Dina, was planning to come along on the bus, but as soon as she heard we were going in the Jaguar instead she changed her mind. She won't sit in the same car as Michel.

But who cares? We're off to the fields where that metal bird's waiting to carry our pals over the big drink! We talk about what fine flying weather it is. Near Aalter, in a slight, almost imperceptible bend in the road, we observe a moment of silence in memory of Toothless John, who fell asleep there one day in his BMW. They had to sweep him up in a dustpan. He was a real demon at rami-bridge, old Toothless John.

But up near Bruges we start laughing again, fit to burst, because over on the right where the pine trees look darker, that's where Rickabone—back in '56, as I recall—drove his DS into a laundry van. The highway patrol had to pull him out from behind the wheel, higher than a kite and no pants on. The two shrieking French girls sitting beside him were naked as shorn poodles, so the laundry man lent them a couple of shirts.

The countryside is pale green. Brand-new factories everywhere, those flat, white boxes with lots of glass, so when you're working you can keep an eye on your car, sitting out there in the parking lot with hundreds of others, like toy cars on a football field.

"What's up, Jake?" asks Rev'em-up Red. "Am I goin' too fast? You feelin' pukey?"

"He's just nervous about the trip," says Michel.

"No," says Jake, "it's 'cause I was in such a hurry I . . ."

"You've been up since six this morning!" says Michel.

"I know, but at the last minute I couldn't find my passport."

"So where's it now, your passport?"

"Right here," says Jake, slapping his breast pocket. "Sonof-abitch!" he cries.

"Tell me it isn't true," moans Michel.

Jake hunts and grunts. "Want me to pull over?" asks Rev'em-up Red.

"Hey! I've got it!"

It was in his shoulder bag. Yes, Jake's bought himself a shoulder bag, after the fashion of all the young men nowadays who'd rather not walk around with bulging pants pockets, or who'd rather have no pockets at all.

"An' I was in such a hurry I forgot to eat," says Jake.

"That's unusual," says Rev'em-up Red, "judgin' from the shape of you."

"I'm all miscombobulated," says Jake.

At the airport he races to the snack bar and gobbles down three rolls with paper-thin slices of boiled ham, while Michel busies himself with the tickets and various other formalities. Rev and I order a beer. Suddenly Jake opens his eyes wide and cries, with his mouth full of ham, "Well, blow me down!"

In the pale green morning light, among the throngs of bewildered tourists (who look a lot more colorful and frivolous than travelers in a railroad station), are three Unicorners, choking with laughter and pointing at us and doing their damndest to belt out "Arrivederci Roma." Our hearts swell with pride when we recognize Markie, the child, Doctor Verbraeken, Markie's father confessor and wet nurse, and the millionaire Salome.

"The three Graces," says Michel. And it's true, we hate to admit it, but the only Unicorners who came to say goodbye are all *of the other persuasion*. With Markie you could see it on TV, when he was cycling, that funny twist of the hips. Salome, who's called that because (among other things) he owns a salami factory, has spent a fortune on young Greeks and Turks. And Doctor Verbraeken takes to the streets some nights dressed as the Queen of Sheba, and it doesn't even have to be Mardi Gras.

"Now, them's what I call friends, goddamit!" growls Rev'em-up Red admiringly, and he rushes toward them. Salome, who's fatter than Jake but has no shoulders, picks Rev up and whirls him around. A paternoster of curses and laughter crackles through the air of the departure lounge, and when Jake goes up to Salome, the millionaire grabs him by the shoulders and booms, "Never thought you'd see us here, did you?"

The tourists, the travelers, are gaping at us like we're a bunch of apes. Markie and Michel shake hands, but their hearts aren't in it. Now we obviously can't keep track of every Unicorn affair, which is why I can only vaguely recall the business between those two. It had to do with some blonde, I believe, who'd jumped in the sack with Markie after he'd won at Bachte-Mariakeerne, and it seems she told Michel that our champ had calves like steel but that the Main Feature was *a joke*. She'd spent ten minutes looking for it! That crazy dingaling Michel went and told everybody, so one night at the Unicorn Markie lays his jack (his real jack!) on the table and shouts: "What d'you call this, a knitting needle?"

Or was it an affair with another lady, a sweet young thing? Yes. Yes indeed. We know who it was, too.

We're not going to say her name out loud. Never. We're not even going to think it. We'd be hurting a certain father if we did. And Rickabone was mixed up in it too, in that filthy affair. Enough! This is one bottle of grief that stays capped.

Markie greets Rev'em-up Red with considerably more enthusiasm. He puckers his lips and rasps out a loud, harsh sputtering.

"Ha!" laughs Rev. "That's a Yamaha 314."

Salome, who has wriggled his sloping shoulders and generous paunch into a houndstooth made-to-measure suit, reaches into his crocodile attaché case and pulls out a bottle of Courvoisier. That's the mark of a true director general, because Salome has a deep blue, thick-lashed, almond-shaped eye for detail, and the main detail at Middelkerke Airport is that there isn't a single bar equipped to handle real world travelers. We drink straight from the bottle.

"Well, you black devil?" says Salome in his rough, sozzled bass.

"Well, what?" asks Michel.

"Aren't you glad we came to say *au revoir*?"

"Sure."

"Then don't make such a face."

"You come here in the Ferrari?" asks Rev'em-up Red. With a pitying smile, Doctor Verbraeken points to the big greasy windows behind him, where Salome's helicopter stands gleaming in the sun.

"They wouldn't let us land at first," says Salome. "So I told that bastard: you give me a decent spot or I'll land on your boss's

gazebo!" Boisterous laughter. "It's too bad this silly thing"—
Salome poked Doctor Verbraeken in the stomach—"has to be at
the hospital in an hour for a tumor, or we could've whisked you
off to England in our chopper!"

You can say what you like about Salome, and it's true he's a Je-
suit when it comes to business affairs and that he owes an awful
lot to the Freemasons, but one thing you can't deny: he's classy.
And so tactful! Because how many bodies would say about their
own helicopter: *our* chopper? Of course, it's also true that the helicopter was bought for Markie, the gentleman's darling, after
he'd won the *Omloop van 't Volk*, to fly him in comfort from one
race to the next, at home and abroad. Winters, to the slopes, and
summers, Saint-Tropez. Meek, pretty Markie. You don't read
much about him in the sports pages these days, things move fast
in the world of heroes and champions, faster down than up.

Doctor Verbraeken gives each of our flyers a bottle of airsick
pills. Which makes Salome's stylishly clad bulk wobble and shake,
he's got to hang onto Markie he's laughing so hard. We laugh too,
just for the fun of it, but it's only when Salome barks at Michel,
"At least those are *real* pills, you little devil!" that we know why
we're laughing. We remember, and let out a whoop. Good God
Almighty, that Michel!

(Because one time at the Unicorn Salome called Michel out
into the courtyard, needed to talk to him. Seems he had a ren-
dezvous with some boy scout, but he was afraid he was going to
have problems, that he wouldn't be able to make the grade, because lately, owing to booze or stress, he just couldn't get it up,
and he needed something foolproof, some kind of medicine, or
maybe a shot, so he'd know for sure that when the time came he'd
be stiff as a crowbar.

"I'd ask Doctor Verbraeken, but he's so jealous he'd tell Markie, and that boy's been so nervous lately he'd make a scene. No, Michel, you're a clever dog, you take care of it for me."

"Don't worry, Salome," says Michel, "I guarantee you the *Eiffel Tower.*"

So Michel brought him back a Coke bottle full of pills from Amsterdam, where they're a lot more advanced in these matters. And it worked. Salome was in seventh heaven. It was Christmas! he told us later. Not once, not twice, but all night long.

Salome was so pleased that, being the dedicated industrialist that he is, he gave one of these pills to a student to analyze so they could mass produce it and he'd be shooting off like a machine gun till he was ninety. You know what's coming, don't you, sir? That's right! Extensive analysis at the university lab showed that the pill contained the very same formula—ABC334 or whatever it was— they use to cure tapeworm in chickens! The Unicorn went wild . . .

"Okay," said Michel, "but did it do the trick?"

"Yes," admitted Salome.

"So what're you complaining about?"

"You're right," said Salome, "I shouldn't be complaining. But if it's all the same to you, Michel, I don't think I'll be taking 'em anymore, those Amsterdamned pills of yours."

Whereupon the denizens of the Unicorn, worn out from all that laughing, had a lively debate about the fact that the wheels of love are fueled by what goes on in the mind, and not in the gear down below.)

The redheaded stewardess beckons, everyone crowds around the departure gate. We've polished off the Courvoisier.

"Want me to give your regards to Dina?"

"If it's not too much trouble. Thanks," says Jake, white as a sheet.

"Drop us a line, eh?" roars Salome. "Don't forget! It's always good for a laugh!"

"Sonofabitch!" Jake races to the souvenir shop and buys a color postcard of Middelkerke beach and a bulbous plastic ballpoint, inside of which you can see the vaulted airport terminal in pink and blue. On the edge of the counter, with Michel grumbling by his side, Jake neatly fills in the card. "Dearest Dina, dearest Didi, we had a Nice Flight. Lots of kisses from Papa."

"But Jake, you haven't left yet!" says Markie.

"Sonofabitch!"

Now you might say, Markie, what does he know, he never even finished summer school, but he's absolutely right. The moment Jake and Michel go up they could come crashing back down again, in a sea of fire, not a Chinaman's chance, and poor old Dina and Didi just sitting there in the parlor and the very last sign of life from their husband and father is a postcard with a scandalous lie, a lie unto death.

We see Jake trying to figure out which of us is the most reliable. He hands his card to Rev'em-up Red and explains that he should listen to the radio, the one o'clock news, and if no planes have crashed, the card can go in the mailbox.

"Don't you worry 'bout a thing," says Rev. We accompany them up to the edge of the tarmac, up to where our fatherland ends. Salome gives them a few last tips on playing poker with Americans. Jake clutches his boarding pass to his chest like a trump card. Michel frowns, as though he'd much rather be going with us to the Casino.

We wave and wave, till we can wave no more.

5

ON BOARD, among the mostly English-speaking passengers, Jake is wedged in his seat like a blond, balding Buddha, his belly three fleshy folds beneath his clothes, the boarding pass clenched in his fist.

"Are you scared?"

"A little," says Jake. "And I can't move." Michel loosens Jake's seatbelt, Michel passes Jake the skimpy cheese-and-tomato sandwiches, Michel explains to Jake that the whole trip is insured for two million francs.

"Does Dina get that, if . . ."

"Sure she does."

"That bitch!" says Jake, and immediately regrets it. "And D-Didi," he stammers. "Does Didi get anything, legally, I mean?"

"Sure she does."

England, below them, is greener than their fatherland. And there are fewer houses.

"Are you sorry?" asks Jake.

"About what?"

"'Bout taking me with you," says Jake quietly.

"Not yet."

"Just wait."

"If you get to be a nuisance, I'll leave you behind and you'll be on your own. Remember that."

Jake leafs through a tiny book with a scarlet cover. "In-doo-*bee*-ta-bleye," he says slowly. "Jeez, I'll never get the hang of this."

"You're supposed to say it like you've got a hot potato in your mouth. In-*dyoo*-bi-teh-blee."

When they land in England, where it's warmer than it was in Europe, Jake tries out his English on the ground stewardess: "How do you do?" She doesn't answer, just grins.

The bus driver who takes their suitcases and carefully slides them into the baggage compartment says "lovely" as he straightens up and dusts off his hands.

In the bus Jake says, "Those English are real charming. 'Lovely' . . . who'd say that in Belgium? To folks he doesn't even know."

They're headed for Rochford. The sign appears along the road. "I thought Roquefort was in France," says Jake.

"Jake."

"Yes?"

"We've got to get one thing straight, you and me. You're not going to act stupider than you already are. Save that for the guys in the Unicorn, they'll fall for it every time. But don't try it with me, not on this trip. It won't work."

"It was a joke," says Jake, startled by this first, almost threatening rebuke.

At Rochford, a little railroad station full of Englishmen, they have to drag their heavy suitcases over an iron bridge. Panting and sweating, Jake stares at the natives. "They're real different, aren't they?"

"How d'you mean, different?"

"Calmer. More polite."

"Look's like you've made a hit," says Michel.

"Who, where?"

Sure enough, a tall, blond teacher, or maybe a head nurse, is giving Jake the eye. Jake mutters under his breath, "Better watch out, ma'am, or I'll grab ya!"

She smiles. She's got freckles and crow's-feet.

"How do you do?" squeaks Jake in his best English.

"I'm fine. Thank you."

"Thank you," says Jake proudly, then goes waddling off after Michel, who has started running, his bags swinging wildly, to the front of the train. The coward.

The empty compartment is covered with dark gray soot. Ten minutes later Jake discovers that there are no doors between the compartments and pisses out the window. Cursing and giggling when he sees the spatters on his pants, he sits back down. "If I had to hold it in all the time I'd have a stiff upper lip, too!"

But soon he starts getting restless. "England's nice and neat with all those old houses, they're lucky they never had a war, but it's pretty boring. How 'bout a game of cards?"

"You just keep your nose in that dictionary," says Michel. "So you'll know what to say when we get to America."

For the next half hour Jake pores over his tiny book; now and again he says something out loud. He keeps waiting for Michel to correct him, but Michel is absorbed in a Royal Air Force magazine.

"Would you look at us, riding through England," says Jake. "Whoever would've thought . . ."

"Me," says Michel.

"Yes, it's all your fault."

"It's more Marianne's fault."

"Who's that?"

"Marianne, the blonde who made that phone call in the Unicorn."

"What's she got to do with our trip?"

At one of the stations along the way an Englishman gets in with a bad case of the sniffles. His tweed suit emits a smell like wet cement.

"A lot," says Michel. "Everything."

"How's that?"

Michel puts down his magazine and looks out at the landscape, rippling and green. "It all began at the Cancan. We wanted to roll some dice and she was sitting at the next table and was dead set on playing. That is to say, her boyfriend wanted to play, and she said: 'Don't think I'm just gonna sit here like a fifth wheel. I'm in.' She had a neckline down to her navel. She used to be Rickabone's sweetheart, too, you know."

"No."

"Yes. In the last few months of his life."

"Rickabone was always popular with the ladies," says Jake.

"Sure, when he was in the money," says Michel, suddenly grim. He picks up his magazine again and starts reading. So that Jake has no choice but to ask:

"And then what happened? At the Cancan?"

"Okay. I say: Okay. What're we playing for? A pint, says her lover boy—who'd shave an egg. No way, she cries, this isn't the boy scouts! The loser pays a bottle of champagne, and if I lose, well . . . then it's a noonie."

"A *noonie?* What's that?"

"I asked her the same thing," says Michel. "Well, she says, if I lose the winner can eat over at my place, not in the evening, but at *noon*—so I ask: Why don't you just call it *lunch?* Or *luncheon,* if you really wanna get formal. Oh, a noonie's more than just lunch, she says, 'cause after lunch we drink a glass of cognac, or two, three, six, seven, whatever you like, and the-e-e-n . . ." Michel lowers a libidinous right eyelid, draws down thick, flaccid lips, sticks out the tip of his tongue and wiggles it.

"Was she pissed?" asks Jake.

"A little. So I say, What about him? Oh, my Freddy? she says. Oh, he doesn't get home from work till five, and you'll be long gone by then. 'Cause after five this is all for my Freddy and no-body else." Michel grabs his chest with both hands, kneads it, shakes it. The English gentleman immediately looks away, snif-fling and grumbling.

"But only if I lose, that is, she says. Otherwise, forget it. Okay, so we throw the dice, she plays like a player, but I throw three sev-ens and win hands down. Marianneke, I say, this is your lucky day, don't try to back out on me now, when and where is our noonie? Anytime you like, she says, here's my address. But not before eleven-thirty."

"Where does she live?" asks Jake. "In the Dampoort?"

It's as if they had never flown over a single channel, as if they aren't on their way to the Promised Land at all, but chained to a card table in the Unicorn, in the reek of knockwurst and ciga-rettes and beer.

"None of your business," says Michel. "Okay. About three days later—thought I'd let her simmer a while, know what I mean?—I ring her bell, around twelve in the afternoon. She answers the door. Hey, look who's here! Michel! Come on in, she says, I've just made coffee. I say: Pardon me, Marianneke, but what I really came for was a glass of wine with my lunch and then a couple of, you know, cognacs. What d'ya mean? she asks. I say: I'm here for my noonie, remember? She goes all pale. Get lost, you pervert, she says. You're lucky my Freddy isn't home, he'd break your face! And then she says, real quietly and red as a beet: Michel, it's all a big misunderstanding. About the noonie, I didn't mean it. I only said it because I'd had one too many and I felt like getting back at my Freddy! It was like a kick in the teeth. What a nerve! And my *dong . . .*"

Michel brings his palm down on his crotch with a furious *whack*. The Englishman snaps open his newspaper and buries himself behind it.

". . . my dong said, So long!"

"I can imagine," says Jake.

"I couldn't get out of there fast enough. But here's the best part—women, I'll never understand 'em!—she's been following me around like a puppy ever since, gazing at me like I'm the Lamb of God . . ." Michel flutters his lashes, widens his eyes, flares his nostrils. ". . . and just waiting for me to attack."

"So, what you're saying is, it's her fault, because of that noonie, that you and me are on our way to America?" asks Jake. "No, sir, there's got to be more to it than that."

"You're right. There is more to it."

"What?"

Michel whips out his *Hitlerjugend* dagger and starts cleaning his nails.

After a while Michel says, "I'll tell you one of these days, when the time is right."

Jake is drowsy. He has seen more than enough of England. He suspects that the reason for their leaving, for Michel's sudden generosity—because a trip like this, even with the charter flight, costs an arm and a leg—has something to do with the fact that

Marianne, so to speak, was Rickabone's last widow. Rickabone, Michel's mirror, emblem, paragon. But Jake would rather not know all the details. Some things are better left alone.

Michel puts his feet up on the worn velvet seat opposite him, which elicits hawking, hacking, and harrumphing from the British skunk. Mama's never been to England, Michel thinks. He tries to look out the grimy window through his mother's hard, light eyes, and it's as if he is turning a knob on his TV set: the landscape grows clear and bright, even the pointy old steeples, the golfers, the sheep. It's unbearable. He taps Jake's thigh with his shoe.

"What did Dina say about me?"

"When?" Jake opens his eyes.

"This morning, before you left?"

"Oh, Dina . . ."

"Didn't she say anything about me at all?"

"She just whined a little."

Michel nods. "Right up to the very last, huh?"

"Yup." I'm being disloyal to Dina, Jake thinks. Why? Because Michel's my friend, he's *got* to be, we're in this together.

He says, "She's been a—a real pain in the ass lately."

"Nothing new about that," says Michel.

"Whenever I want to go to the movies, she says: Aw, come on, stay home. When I'm watching TV, a French comedy or something like that, she says: How can you watch anything so stupid?"

"What're you supposed to watch?" Michel asks impatiently.

"Something educational, she says. Whenever we go camping, all I hear is: Jake, haven't you put up the tent yet? If we take Didi on a picnic, it's: Jake, don't tell me you brought blutwurst again! Morning till night, Michel, morning till—"

"How much longer's this going to go on, Jake?"

Desire

"Till the day she dies," says Jake, and his betrayal sounds like rage, when in fact it's meant purely to please Michel, to gratify him in his loathing for Dina. "Till the day she goddamn dies!" barks Jake into the thick tweedy stench of the Englishman behind his *Times*.

6

IN LONDON, under the blazing sun, Jake stands outside the ultramodern Palace Cinema Complex waiting for Michel.

Opposite him, in the little square park beneath the skyscrapers, shirt-sleeved Londoners are sitting on benches fanning themselves. The younger ones are sprawled, half naked, in the grass.

"Boy, do I feel like a moron," Jake mutters to himself. "He promised not to leave me behind unless I got to be a nuisance. But I haven't been a nuisance at all. We've been getting along fine. Guess he changed his mind, I've been waiting here more than three-quarters of an hour. No, he's gone too far this time. If I don't move, just stand perfectly still, everything'll turn out fine. And the sweat, God, I can feel it running down my face into my neck. It's from those six different kinds of Indian food Michel made us order. All those spices. One bite and your whole body's on fire, but you keep on eating 'cause it tastes so good and it's not every day you get stuff like that in Belgium, mango, tandoori, must be hell on your innards but it's still pretty interesting, though once is enough. I'm broiling out here, but if I go stand in the shade Michel'll never show up. The Indian guy who owned the restaurant welcomed us in like prodigal sons. Smiling and smiling with that big yellow apricot face of his. He put a glass of water down in front of me and said, 'Thank-you very much.' Pretty funny. I said, 'I'll have a beer, please.' But that wasn't allowed. Soda water, no problem. You can't get wine or beer in London, except in pubs and then only at certain times. And they call themselves a metropolis! And that traffic on the wrong side of the street. Scares the living daylights out of me. Good thing we're only spending one night here. If Michel doesn't show up in the next ten minutes I'm going home. First back to the hotel. But what was the name of that hotel? And where was it? We drove here in a cab. Michel said, 'You go into town without me, I've got some business to take care of.' I'll bet he does. Probably smuggled something over on the plane. I'm going back home, to Belgium. But how? I've got no English money and he's got my passport."

A guy with a beard and an Elvis T-shirt edges up to Jake. Very casually, without looking at him once, he starts rubbing together his thumb and index finger. Can Jake spare some change? Jake turns white as a sole's belly.

"Go away," says Jake, "or I'll beat you stupider than you already are."

The guy with the beard won't leave him alone. He moves even closer. Jake sees the boils in his neck, the knurled red ears, and he peers over the bum's shoulder to the main street, through the railings of the fence around the park, but no taxi pulls up, no breathless, sweaty Michel comes running.

This bearded character has a tic. One side of his face creeps slowly upward, forms wrinkles, and then, all at once, drops back down again.

"Go," says Jake. "Go," and he points threateningly to a steaming grate. The man traipses off, all alone in the world. (Him too. No, not me. There's Didi. I'm sweating like a pig. Michel's probably gotten mixed up in some awful business. I can't help him. There are lots of Turks in London. Or maybe they're Indians. They walk around like they belong here, don't give a damn what anybody thinks. Not like back home. *Our* Turks know their place, they stick to their own shops, their own pubs, where it always stinks of that foul tobacco.)

Standing opposite the dazzlingly lit entrance to the Palace is a girl in a black turban. She, too, is waiting for some unfaithful cad. (Should I go up to her? What would I say? Hey, doll, you just washed your hair? Or are you bald?) Jake feels a headache coming on. Sunstroke?

The man in the box office, Jake notices, is also enjoying the spectacle. Yes, sir, a new world record is being set here today, the Longest Wait in History! You see before you an innocent man being roasted alive while, at this very moment, the woman he's waiting for is writhing in the greasy, hairy arms of a Turk!

There's no oxygen in this city. The foursquare towers with their vehement billboards trap the heat like a cloud of smoke between their walls, between the crowds of hurried, harried, unintelligible strangers. (If Dina could see me now. She'd laugh. She never laughs so hard as when somebody's making a fool out of me. Laugh, Dina. I don't blame you. The sun'll set, the moon'll rise, and I'll still be standing here.) Jake curses.

A taxi pulls up outside the Palace, but the door opens on the other side, for the girl in the turban. A fat woman beckons to the girl, who steps into the cab without so much as a glance at Jake, her partner in humiliation, in desperate expectation.

Rickabone often said, "If every man spent two years in a monastery, he'd learn enough patience and mortification to last him the rest of his life." We'd say, "So why don't you, Rickabone?" "One of these days . . ." he'd sigh.

When Michel finally shows up, looking perfectly calm and collected, he explains to Jake, "I fell asleep in the movie theater but I didn't have my watch, and all of a sudden I woke up and *raced* outside, but I couldn't get a cab! I ran all the way here."

"I don't see you sweating," says Jake.

"Yeah, well, I was almost here and I got these shooting pains in my spleen and I had to slow down. I'm sure glad to see you. I thought: He's going to be so mad he'll go straight back to the hotel."

"I didn't know where the hotel was," says Jake.

"Didn't you take one of those address cards? They were on the front desk!"

"Nope," says Jake. Once again it's his own stupid fault. "What you just did, you wouldn't dare do that with anybody else."

"That's what you think," says Michel, with an impish grin. He looks five years younger.

In the cab back to the hotel he tells Jake that he's been to a porno movie, pictures of which, in the glass case outside, promised a pair of monstrously fat nurses in various states of arousal. But what a letdown! There was no air-conditioning, the picture was out of focus, the women were too skinny, you could see their ribs, which was fine for a glossy, but not for serious porn, and besides, Michel still hadn't gotten over the flight, because if you stopped to think about it they *had* crossed a whole sea . . .

"Why couldn't I go with you to the movies? Why did you tell me you still had some business to take care of?"

"Oh, you know how it is. If it's really good porn and you're all turned on, you feel kind of embarrassed if someone you know is sitting there watching you, and if it's lousy, you feel embarrassed 'cause you made your buddy go with you."

"Was it that bad?"

"It was in color. That's always bad."

They're staying at the Hotel Londonderry, a two-story house in a shoddy side street. The concierge, an eighteen-year-old with earrings and oiled eyelids, is standing in the narrow, pale green corridor watching a cricket match on TV. Jake turns the rack of postcards, which gives an earsplitting squeak, and the concierge snarls something at him. "Yes, sir," says Jake.

The tiny window in their cubbyhole of a room won't open. On the wall is a painting of a wild boar, which looks as if it's floating through the air, because it casts no shadow and its hooves don't touch the ground. Jake says: "That's the boar in the painter's dream."

"That's Dina talking," says Michel.

The standing lamp between their beds is speckled with fly shit. In the room next door, an old man is singing a polka. Jake and Michel play manille till deep in the night. After that Michel doesn't sleep a wink. Jake snores, grinds his teeth, and every now and then he mutters something. "Pie," Michel thinks he hears. Or was it "Thigh"?

When a grayish light begins to dawn, Michel tugs at Jake's shirt. "Come on."

"It's too early. The cab won't be here till seven."

"So we'll go out and hail our own. Be a lot cheaper, too." Suddenly the sun's up, warm against the peeling, pastel-colored house fronts. Jake's eyelids are blood red, as if he's been crying all night long.

7

THE PLANE HAS THREE ENGINES, costs twenty million dollars, and has two hundred and seventy men and women on board, plus the crew, and twelve stewardesses wearing plaid skirts made of some coarse material that makes them look six months pregnant.

Jake breaks the headset (with its in-flight selection of classical, jazz, easy listening, country and rock) by squashing it down on his skull like a helmet. Staring fixedly out the window, he pokes the broken plastic twig in his ear and tunes in to *Ernani*, by Verdi.

Michel looks like thunder. The stewardess, the pretty one with the cool, sleek, confident air, has seated them (no doubt with an eye to Jake's Herculean proportions) in the first row, where you've certainly got more leg room, but where they also hang up the coats, just opposite them, so that every five minutes some son-ofabitch on his way to America comes over to rummage around in his own or other people's pockets.

Gatwick Airport was a lot farther than Michel had expected. They pounced on the first available cab, but the fuzzy-haired Papuan behind the wheel took them down all the wrong streets. Out of malice, perhaps. Or sheer stupidity.

And Jake has been unbearably cheerful, raving about the stewardesses' backsides, the free smoked almonds, the flocks of sheep you could see when the plane took off, just briefly, like the corner of an old painting.

They very nearly missed the plane, too, because after they had obediently taken their place at the back of a line of English-speaking tourists in Hawaiian shirts, a goggle-eyed calf in a uniform told them it was the wrong gate. "So which gate is it, you goat?" yelled Michel, but all she said was "Not this one," and they went hurtling down the wide, sunstruck corridors like two maniacs, shouting questions at anything in uniform, but nobody knew and there wasn't an escalator in sight. They were the very last to arrive; the crew was chomping at the bit. Right now Michel could swallow a whole bottle of aspirin, but that's dangerous, aspirin's bad for the kidneys. He can see himself sitting next to his mother in her cauliflowered kitchen, dialysis twice a week, Mama flushing out his kidneys with a slimy rubber tube.

"Take off your shoes." Jake doesn't want to. Has he got holes in his socks?

"Take off your jacket." Jake doesn't want to.

"You can smoke if you want." Jake doesn't want to, doesn't dare to, he just sits there, paralyzed with fear. Only when the food arrives does he unwind. He eats half of Michel's tray, too, spilling wine on his sweater, of course. The ugly stewardess, the one with the underbite, wants him to give her the sweater so she can clean it, probably stick it under the faucet in the restroom, but Jake doesn't want to.

"Tell her clothes like these have to go to the dry cleaners," he whispers.

Michel translates, saying that his uncle never takes off his sweater during the day, only before going to sleep, or, ahem, an intimate encounter.

The ugly stewardess smiles compassionately.

The pretty stewardess keeps a safe distance from the first row. She has broad cheekbones, a smoothly gleaming, flawless complexion, flaxen hair combed back into an improbably tight bun. She wears the huge chrome-plated safety pin, which holds together the inelegant tartan skirt, higher up than the other stewardesses, so that every time she moves you get a glimpse of thigh.

Michel calls her over and orders two double cognacs. World traveler. Jake wants to know where the engines are. In the tail, she says. Jake shrieks with laughter. "Same as me!"

Do they have horse racing in America? She doesn't know. Overwhelmed, desperate, the pretty stewardess tells them she has other passengers to attend to. "No," says Jake, and immediately orders two more double cognacs, asks what region they're flying over, how high they're flying, how much a pilot earns. The pretty stewardess flees.

"Wait until dark!" Jake cackles.

Michel snaps his fingers, the ugly stewardess reappears. When's the next meal? How much does a stewardess earn? Who was Ernani?

"Ernani?"

"What? You put it on your program, you blast it in people's ears, and you don't even know what it's about? *Ernani*, by Giuseppe Verdi!"

The ugly stewardess promises to provide them with all the information they need, but first she has to take a little deaf-mute to the potty.

"Now that's what I call service!" says Michel, and he's drunk, almost happy. "You still scared?"

"Me? It's like sitting in my own living room!" says Jake.

In Jake's living room, two feet away from his nose, a white

screen drops down and the movie begins. You can't understand a word of what the cowboys and Indians are yelling at each other, but there's plenty of wild music, trampling hooves, and creaking wagon wheels. You see the Indian (a nice enough young man if you don't get in his way) drawing white chalk marks all over his brawny chest, 'cause he's going on the warpath! White soldiers have set fire to his hut and burned his only son to a crisp.

"They used to have wigwams," says Jake. "Remember?"

The major in the dark blue uniform is sulking because some lone, lithesome Apache (in the moonlight you couldn't tell if it was the vengeful young father) has, in a soundless flash, slit the throat of a sentry. "Men," he says grimly to a row of craggy old warhorses, "I wanna see scalps before sundown!"

The screen is too close, the huge faces are craters of crimson lava, colors and gestures flow together, Jake and Michel slump shoulder to shoulder, breathe in each other's faces, turn away in annoyance, slump back together again.

"I'm dead," says Michel several hours later.

"I'm worse."

"Why don't you walk around a little?"

"Am I allowed? Maybe you're only allowed to walk around the plane at certain times. Look. Everybody else is asleep . . ."

"Walk around," orders Michel.

"Hey, you don't have to be so rude," says Jake. He has never been this high up, this far above the clouds, this close to the stars. The floor below his feet feels thin, brittle.

The night, usually so full, so lingeringly strange and bursting with visions and dreams, now lasts an hour at most, the windows are light and clear, and look, the sun's coming up! The pretty stewardess drifts over and stands next to him. "Have a seat," says Jake, and she perches one buttock on his armrest. Is he German?

Jake stares incredulously at the perfect, smooth-toned face, the curled lashes, the glazed red lips. "*Nein*, no German!" says Jake. It sounds like an order from a customs officer. "My father was German," she says apologetically, and drifts away.

(I'm no good with women, Michel's much better at it. Didi's not a woman.)

Michel wakes up with drooping eyelids and a dark shadow over cheeks and chin. He says they better stick to blackjack, once they get to America. The rules are the same as twenty-one, only you've got blackjack and that's when . . .

"I need to see it before I can understand it," says Jake.

Cognac in the clear, glorious light of dawn. Children run up and down the aisles, yipped at by exhausted mothers. The pilot says something scientific about the polar circle and dips down to show them the icescape. The stewardesses bustle around with pills and drinks and sandwiches.

Michel explains why air hostesses are so incredibly horny. Seems their glands and nerves are always getting scrambled together by mysterious transitions in time and space.

"You mean, like it's always a full moon?" asks Jake.

"Exactly."

Jake concentrates on the ugly stewardess, the only one to have donned a cap with a pom-pom. Could this be a sign that she is now approachable, seducible, that in just a few moments she'll kneel down between the coat rack and Flemish knees and allow herself to be fondled, pawed, soiled, bruised?

Jake snaps his fingers, as loudly and efficiently as Michel, but she doesn't come. Jake waves to her as if she's selling ice cream at a soccer game, but she must be nearsighted.

"Lady, lady!" cries Jake, and, wonder of wonders, she starts moving toward him through the odorless (no, he smells ozone) cabin of the shimmering, ice gold star-spangled DC 10.13. Oiled, functional, a roguish look in her eye, she approaches in all her tartan glory, with her potbelly, her underbite (from kissing too many world travelers), and Jake says, or thinks he does, "Madame, of all the madames that fly through the air, you are the fairest of them all."

What he really says is, "Lady, I love you."

She laughs, without making a sound. Jake nudges Michel.

"Tell her I think she's pretty."

Michel translates: "My uncle thinks you're hot."

"You want a punch in the mouth?" snarls Jake. "I know what you said!"

"That's all right," says the stewardess.

"And I'm not his uncle. I'm not even related to him. I know him from the pub, that's all," says Jake.

"All right," she says firmly.

Jake grabs her hand and kisses it. She looks quickly from side to side before pulling it back. "You're sweet," she says and disappears into First Class.

"Now she'll tell the pilot," says Michel. "And he'll radio it down to Los Angeles. There'll be a whole police force waiting for us at the airport."

"She wouldn't do a thing like that," says Jake. He curls his lip up to his nose. "She could try washing her hands, though," he says triumphantly.

Michel blinks. Is this the Jake he knows, the sluggish, sheepish giant who sits in the Unicorn between courtyard and bar? It's as though Jake's blubber has grown firmer, more resilient. And there's a note of gaiety, of playful defiance, in his high-pitched voice. (How the hell am I going to tame him?)

"I feel like doing something silly."

"Control yourself."

Jake looks down at the handle under glass, under the red metal plate: Exit lift handle. *Galida levante la manija.*

"Don't touch that," says Michel.

"I feel kind of drunk, you know? Not from the booze. It's the air in here. There's too much oxygen, or maybe too little. Or is it carbon dioxide?"

But soon Jake is thoroughly absorbed in peeling off the plastic wrap from his tray of food, the butter, the salt, the dairy creamer, the kiddie-sized silverware, the mustard. After drinking all his orange juice and bolting down the watery corn, leathery chicken, and apple pie, he drops off to sleep: open mouth, three filled molars, and a coated tongue. Now and again his pale lashes tremble. The plastic tube dangling from his ear plays Linda Ronstadt singing "The Sweetest Gift." Then his turgid bulk heels over, the double-chinned head drops, seeks a pillow, finds Michel's shoulder.

The dawn was a lie, the sun has disappeared, the windows are flocky and gray. Michel, his nose buried in Jake's hair, dozes off, wakes with a start, and is once again caught unawares by the murmur of the engines. The enormous polyp that drifts through the galaxy and has enwrapped the plane in manifold strands of gossamer sticks out one of its tongues and licks the cockpit, hungry suckers fix themselves to the shuddering fuselage and hundred-gilled arms swish past the wings through the rarified air, and now, now, a bulging, bloodless, implacably glassy eye scrapes along the dull window and sticks there, right in my face, I'm sleeping, I'm protecting Jake, can't you see me cradling his fragile head?—but the tentacles coil gently and malevolently around the clattering tailplanes, the DC 10.13 is out of control, nothing to be done, we're going down, distant control towers jabber and quack,

Michel screams his pleas to the inescapably luminous mollusc of an eye at the window, the undercarriage sinks, miraculously, the nosewheel dives, hits, bounds and twirls, spewing passengers like cockroaches, baobabs splinter, old women shriek, the plane shatters into a million pieces.

Michel jerks upright, drenched with sweat; Jake topples over.

"My ears hurt," says Jake. "Didn't Doctor Verbraeken give us pills for that?"

"Go back to sleep," Michel says. Orders. *Demands.* Jake obeys.

To his amazement Michel sees that next to the window, at shoulder height, is a narrow crack. And through this crack in the shell of the crate (as planes are known in aviation circles, Michel heard that once on a game show), water is seeping in. He vaguely remembers the gushing tears of the great polyp, just moments before.

Jake, too, is amazed. He utters mouselike squeaks of indignation. What? *Our* plane? Is *our* plane leaking, like some old shed? "Lady, lady!"

The ugly stewardess explains that the leak is caused by a layer of ice that has formed on the body of the plane. She runs a cloth around the edges of the window, while the plane lies on its side and shivers.

Then Jake asks what's more dangerous, taking off or landing. "Landing," says the stewardess, as she fusses about with bags, coats, blankets.

"Ooooooh . . ." Jake squeezes his eyes shut, grabs the faded, shapeless pillow behind his neck and crams it into his mouth.

All of a sudden he's surrounded by giggling, jostling passengers. He hears dance music, thin and sweet.

"How high are we? When does the landing start?"

"Fathead," says Michel.

"Give me one of those pills. For the landing."

"We've already landed, fathead!"

"What?" Jake jumps to his feet and begins shoving aside the other passengers with his mighty flanks, his granite belly.

Those meteorologists down at the Unicorn who predicted that they'd be burned alive upon arrival didn't know what they were talking about. California is soft, mild, balmy. Jake buttons up his stained vest, he bows (the perfect gentleman) to the pretty stewardess, and then the ugly one, Good night, he says, and walks down the metal staircase with an unworldly, wide-eyed gaze, *ecstatic*, Michel thinks, like a cyclist crossing the finish line in the Tour de France, and then he staggers, that Flemish Giant, his knees give way, his balding head drops onto his chest, he sinks down and, like a pilgrim in the Middle East, he touches his forehead to the tarmac and squeaks, "America, America!"

When the stewardesses and porters rush forward to help he waves them away, laughing, but offers no resistance when Michel hauls him to his feet. "What do you think you're doing, you idiot?"

"It's just like Christopher Columbus," says Jake. He leans heavily on Michel's shoulders and, with a slight limp, yet more briskly and cheerfully than any of the other passengers, he heads for the airport bus.

In the bus, next to the disheveled travelers who cling wearily to their leather straps, he holds his canvas bag in front of his stomach, to hide, as Michel can see out of the corner of his eye, an all too obvious erection. Jake sees that Michel has noticed.

"Behave yourself," says Michel.

"I can't help it," says Jake. "I'm just so glad to be on the ground."

"Can't you get rid of it?"

"How?" asks Jake, and then, "They can't put me in jail for this, can they?"

What Michel wasn't prepared for, are the palm trees. This could be Egypt. They wander over to the low, ocher yellow buildings.

A jet-black Negress in butterfly glasses inspects their passports. "Oh, Belgium," she says. "You still got a civil war goin' on over there, you poor things?"

"Hunh? What? I haven't been listening to the radio," says Jake. "Since when?"

"Been goin' on a coupla years now, hasn't it?" She scratches Michel's passport with a violet fingernail. "I thought you all were killin' each other off, the Flemings against the Walloons, bomb attacks, that kinda thing?"

"Oh, yes," says Michel quickly. "It's terrible."

Suddenly she says, in a painfully bored tone of voice: "Business or pleasure?"

"Pleasure!" cries Jake. "Much much pleasure!" and rubs, without the least bit of embarrassment, in a way he would never, ever dare in his fatherland, the fearsome bulge in his pants.

"Get *rid* of it," snarls Michel.

"But why?" says Jake, stunned. "It's a sign of good health!"

To Michel's exasperation Jake keeps his hand on his crotch. Michel shoves Jake up against the counter so those butterfly eyes can't land on his weapon.

"*Merci*, Madame," says Jake when he gets his passport back. She responds testily with the advice that he would be better off speaking English in "our country."

"Why certainly," says Jake, and when he gets to the revolving door he shouts what he shouts out every Sunday to the ancient, weary, bald-headed black who sells licorice and peppermint toffee on the bleachers at the soccer stadium, the name that the old man himself screeches over and over like a hoarse parrot: "Carabooya Bamboola!"

"You're welcome," says Madame Butterfly.

8

LOOKING DOWN FROM THEIR FOURTH-FLOOR WINDOW, Michel sees that Jake's immense, paper-white body, lying on an air mattress next to the motel swimming pool, is a great source of amusement to the staff and the five little black kids who are splashing around in the Turkish blue water. Jake is asleep. As soon as he hung up all his clothes, just as he had promised Dina he would, he rushed out to the pool. He's been lying in the sun for three quarters of an hour now, and by tonight he'll be covered with blisters. Michel would like nothing better, but his malice quickly fades when he realizes what a burden this would be.

He walks, past the blacks dressed in white who are busily folding linen, to the poolside. Nothing has gone the way he expected it to. The sky isn't picture-postcard blue after all, but filthy gray (even though the sun is shining!). The taxi that brought them to the motel wasn't a gleaming, luxurious limousine, but a dented, rusty VW, the kind only artistes and other dregs of society would be caught dead in back home. The motel they were driven to by somebody's grandma with a light blue permanent doesn't show porno movies twenty-four hours a day on TV, as Salome had solemnly assured them. Because it was that lying industrialist who gave them the address of the Parliament Motel in the first place. And it's in a suburb, would you believe! Though come to think of it, the whole damn city seems to be made up of suburbs.

Two fat black matrons lower themselves carefully into the pool. Still wearing their voluminous dresses, which float about them like brightly colored lily pads, they splash water at each other and squeal and shout with their offspring. Why have they kept their clothes on? For religious reasons?

Michel sits down in the shade. Jake's overexposed body against a backdrop of natives and palm trees reminds him of the equally bloated white body of Gerald, Rev 'em-up Red's brother, as it appeared on TV several years earlier. Kantangese soldiers in army fatigues lugged the Flemish mercenary, who been slain by the Simbas, all the way across a steamy jungle on a stretcher. The procession was accompanied by machine-gun fire. Every so often they'd drop the body, because they heard the enemy approaching, or because they'd slipped in the mud, or gotten their feet tangled in the bushes. Then Gerald's corpse (Jake's snoring carcass) would go swaying along once more. It was twice the size of the sturdiest Kantangese. Now and again they raised it above their dark heads, like an offering to the snaky lianas and dancing sunspots.

In order to recover from the flight, this new world, their surroundings, and to put off exploring Los Angeles for as long as possible, Jake and Michel play cards. The colors on their TV screen are screamingly bright; they've turned off the sound. They drink up everything in the fridge, Budweiser, the King of Beers for a hundred years, Miller, a distinguished beer with full-bodied taste, Schlitz, a unique and flavorful beer, Jim Bean, a timeless gift, made with the purest glacial spring water, ginger ale (yuck!), Pepsi and Windsor, a classic Canadian whiskey with the smooth flavor you expect and a price you don't. By the time they're finished, it's dark outside.

What the hell is wrong with the United States of America? Jake and Michel walk down the street, down the wide, wide streets of Los Angeles, supposedly the busiest, unhealthiest, most degenerate and crime-ridden and lascivious and overcrowded city in the whole New World, and there isn't a soul in sight.

They walk for three quarters of an hour, toward the illuminated skyscrapers in the distance, and see only six cars. Have the Chinese got some silent, chemical, deadly weapon aimed at this city?

Jake wants to go back to the motel, he's afraid they'll lose their way.

"This is nothing," says Michel. "In Egypt I walked out two miles into the desert, all by myself."

"Okay, but it's your fault if we have to sleep on a bench."

"Quit whining!" Then they get to Broadway and finally see people. Or rather, Mexicans, blacks, winos, and cops, mooning about in a cloud of spices, hot fat, and sweet tobacco.

A seven-foot pimp in a skintight, white leather suit and cowboy boots offers them a pair of genuine young virgins. Michel pulls Jake away by the sleeve.

"I just wanted to find out what the prices are around here."

"The price is a knife in your gut," says Michel.

Whiskey and beer do wonders for the appetite. Jake and Michel duck into a little Mexican restaurant. On their table is a plaster madonna in a rainbow-colored coat. Behind Michel on the wall are posters for boxing matches held twenty years ago. After pointing helplessly to something on the menu, they're served enchiladas and frijoles, white beans in a tepid, gluey sauce, stringy meat, watery tomatoes, and peppers.

"Well, well," says Jake, wiping his plate clean with a cold tortilla and glancing around the room at the grunting half-breeds. "Pretty sleazy, huh?"

"I thought this was right up your alley," says Michel.

"When it comes to women, they can't be sleazy enough. But a restaurant's got to be clean."

Jake reaches for Michel's nearly untouched plate and starts mashing up the beans.

"Hey, hey, watch it with those beans!" cries Michel. "Don't forget, we're sleeping in the same room tonight!"

"It's a free country," says Jake, and takes a huge bite. And laughs, a rebellious guffaw. Michel gulps down his ice cold beer. His knees are shaking. He'd like to plunge his fork into Jake's cheek.

They have no trouble finding their way back and end up in that desolate, ominous zone between the high-rise buildings. All at once, from a gloomy side street, they hear a raucous yell. Michel breaks into a run, without looking back at Jake, without a single word or cry. Jake can't keep up with him, has to slow down, and suddenly there's no more Michel, not even the sound of his footsteps.

"Michel!" screams Jake, and stumbles along the pavement, holding onto his sloshing belly with both hands. After a few blocks he gets a stitch in his side and has to stop. He sits down on the bluestone doorstep of a couturier.

From way up in the air, where it hangs like a red star, an insect descends, rasping and rattling. Jake cringes, a helicopter swings around and hovers between the metal towers, a searchlight plays on the doorway where Jake has run for cover, then sweeps back up into the air.

Sirens moan, animal-like. Then there's silence, or nearly, an electric rumbling, shuffling footsteps, rubber on concrete.

Jake heads for the motel. His feet are killing him. He recognizes the supermarket, the deserted shopping mall with the palm trees, the empty cigarette machine, the lifeless motel with the billboards.

Back in their room Michel is lying in bed watching a huge fire on TV: clouds of soot, waving niggers, shrieking ambulances. Jake undresses in silence; the air-conditioner rustles.

"Are you mad at me?" he asks.

"Me? No."

"Then why did you run away? What'd I do wrong?"

"It was Markie," says Michel, turning away from the crackling TV screen. "Didn't you recognize his voice?"

Jake hesitates. "Now that you mention it . . ."

"Markie's followed us here."

"In the helicopter?"

"Of course not. A helicopter can't fly across the ocean. No. The next plane. And he must've gotten our address from Salome. He's been chasing after us all this time, all evening, and . . ." Michel is driving at something, he's made up this whole, stupid, crazy story. He sits there leering at Jake as if he's holding a preposterous trump card. Jake crawls slowly out of bed and double-locks the door.

"Idiot," says Michel. "You almost fell for it, too."

9

At five the next morning, Michel, against his better judgment, is fiddling with all the knobs on the TV set and cursing Salome because he can't conjure a single porno movie out of this goggle box.

Jake lies curled up in his shorts, like a big fat baby that has been plunked down on the orange bedspread by a giantess. He hasn't moved a muscle in the past hour, even though a normal person, scientists say, is supposed to change position more than thirty times in a single night.

Michel switches on the news. The images on the screen are stippled, the fire in the ghetto is orange and blue, the firemen are lavender shadows, pink blankets are tossed over the bodies, a few of the smoldering walls are forest green.

Jake sits up and drinks a Pepsi, leaning on one elbow. He shakes his head pityingly; his jowls quiver.

"Look," he says. "They're digging those folks out with a shovel."

The anchorman says there are more than thirty dead, and the next moment the screen is filled with strawberry-stippled, lissome young girls frolicking about in a foaming surf, playing tennis and dancing in nightclubs, all because they use Tampax.

Outside there isn't a breath of wind. They walk past the sharp-edged, rectangular houses, past the palms. In a coffeeshop Jake eats what the black lady in curlers recommends, pancakes and sausage, toast dripping with butter, hash browns. "Fried potatoes, at seven o'clock in the morning!" cries Jake delightedly. "Wait'll I tell Dina!"

"Doesn't Dina ever tell you you're too fat?"

"Every day," says Jake. "But if she thinks I'm going to let her ruin my life . . ."

"And Didi?" Michel says her name awkwardly.

"What about Didi?" Jake notices that he, too, has trouble saying her name.

"What does she think of being stuck with an elephant for a father?"

"She doesn't mind."

"That's what *you* think!"

"Let's talk about something else," says Jake, licking the syrup from his fingers and wiping them off on his pants.

Their discovery of America begins at 10 A.M., in a bus that takes them past the baseball stadium, the botanical gardens, a cemetery, and the Homes of the Stars. The driver slows down in front of the immaculate lawns, where Cadillacs and Rolls-Royces gleam, and shouts out the exotic names of flowers and plants, as if he's trying to sell them. The Homes of the Stars look surprisingly alike. Jake can hardly tell them apart, nor can he keep track of all the other names the driver shouts out, of gangsters, guitar players, alcoholics, cowboys, detectives, air force majors, and explorers who have populated the silver screen over the years and whom Dina always recognizes, without even checking the TV guide.

Jake promises himself not to forget the mansion where, at this very moment, wasting away on the third floor, is Jimmy Durante, the man whose nose was insured for two million dollars back in the days when he was still prancing around singing "Rink, a-dink-a-dink, a-dink-a-do." And there's a fake castle choked with ivy where some movie star has been hiding out since 1924, when they botched up her facelift—what was her name again? Not Doris Day, but something like that.

When it comes time for the travelers to stretch their legs and empty their bladders, the bus stops outside a concrete-and-steel amphitheater, the Hollywood Bowl, which the driver says can hold up to twenty thousand people and four thousand cars. On summer nights they do symphonies here, complete with fireworks and booming cannons. The property is valued at three million dollars. That's some bandstand! thinks Jake.

Jogging along the beach, in track suits or stripped to the waist, in running shoes or barefoot, are The Americans. It's the latest craze, says the driver.

"You've got to be nuts," says Jake, "pushing yourself like that. You could bust your spleen!"

After they've been to a Chinese theater and seen where Marilyn Monroe (who, as everyone knows, never wore panties) pressed her fingers, rounded knees, and spike heels into the cement on a July day in 1953, Jake and Michel go traipsing down Hollywood Boulevard. Not a café in sight. They feel more dead than alive; the flight over from Europe has crossed all the wires in their nervous systems.

They wander into a cool, dark bar.

"What'll it be, Jake?" asks Michel.

"Anything, as long as it's beer," says Jake. "Sonofabitch!" he shouts after the first gulp, which, much to the annoyance of the

75

barkeeper, who just happens to look up from his newspaper, he spits out on the floor. "You . . . you bastard!"

"You said anything, as long as it's beer!"

"This isn't beer!"

"Sure it is. Root beer. Made from roots. All natural."

"No," says Jake. "There are limits!"

(A long time ago, the year that everyone was riding around on Vespas, Jake and Rickabone were hanging out one afternoon in Mocambo's. That was the last time he had drunk anything this bad.

"Try some," Rickabone urged. He did, and spit it right out again.

"Coca-Cola," said Rickabone. "The whole world's going to be drinking it."

"No," said Jake. "I don't care how much they advertise, I don't care how hard they try to get it down people's throats, this rat poison'll never sell, no sir. You think a real Belgian would give up his beer for *this?*"

"You're such a child, Jacob," said Rickabone. "It's not a matter of taste.")

Three men are sitting at the bar watching a team of overfed baseball players on TV. One of them turns around; he has a pock-marked face, a wild look in his eyes.

"Where're you guys from?"

"From Belgium," says Jake.

"Hey, where they wear those wooden shoes, right?"

"Yes, that's right," says Michel quickly.

"First time here?"

"Yes," says Michel.

"How d'ya like it?"

"Strange," Jake mutters. "Really str—"

"Beautiful," Michel interrupts him.

"Beautiful," echoes the man, rubbing his chest in the faded T-shirt. "You're damn right about that. This is the greatest country on earth. And we're gonna keep it that way, goddamit!" He waits for a response, then turns back to the TV screen and starts cursing at the players.

Jake and Michel sit around the bar until the lights go on in the street.

"Chesty Morgan . . ." Michel murmurs. "Rickabone used to carry a picture of her in his wallet. If I knew she was performing anywhere within miles of here, I'd race right over, even if it cost me ten thousand francs for a cab. You've got no idea, pal, she's out of this world. Remember that name, Jake, *Chesty Morgan.* Rickabone's dream. Those tits of hers, they're like soccer balls. No, watermelons. No, not even watermelons. It's like they've been transplanted from a twenty-foot woman, from some other species! She's got a silver star stuck to each nipple. She stands there in the spotlight, and when the music starts warming up—organ, usually, kind of classical—those boobs start moving, real slow, from left to right, buddy, side to side, the organ plays faster, they add a couple of trumpets, and while she, Chesty Morgan, and all the rest of her body, her bleached-blond baby face and her powdered shoulders and her narrow waist, stand perfectly still, her boobs start swinging faster too, back and forth, and then, pal, then, I swear on my mother's grave—"

"Your mother's not dead, is she?" asks Jake softly.

"That's a saying, you idiot. Okay, I swear on my mother's wheelchair, those bazoomas start flying in *opposite directions,* the left one goes left and the right one goes right and then they fly together, wham! And then apart, and then they smack together again, you can *hear* 'em, and all that time the rest of her doesn't budge, just those udders, they've got *a life of their own*, that's no exaggeration, buddy, and you remember how Rickabone used to say that women are the source of all things and that we're just a load of blowflies that crawl on top of them to die? Well, he must've been talking about Chesty Morgan, 'cause after that she does exactly the opposite of what she just did, her hips start wiggling under this lacy fringe, back and forth, left to right, and her belly with the diamond in the middle starts rippling up and down, in and out, and her knees and thighs are spreading apart and shaking, like somebody's blasting 'em with a blow drier, but the whole time, Jake, the whole goddamn time, those gleaming, sweaty tits stay put, they hang right down, like they're nailed there, like they're frozen solid . . ."

"You say this lady does a show around here?"

"That's the problem, nobody knows where she is. Rickabone even phoned her agent about it, cost him a fortune. Turns out she disappeared one day, just like that, and nobody's heard from her since, not even her own mother."

"Maybe she's going under a different name," says Jake drunkenly.

"You think so?" Michel's beer glass hovers in midair, he drops his lower lip, blinks his eyes. "That's what Rickabone said, too. He thought maybe she woke up one day and realized she'd gotten too old to spend the rest of her life as Chesty Morgan, 'cause she had wrinkles on her belly, or her butt sagged, and she just didn't want to perform anymore as that, that incredible, that fucking *miracle* . . ."

"You're drunk."

"But Jesus, the thought of her having wrinkles, or pimples . . ."

"So what if she does?" asks Jake.

". . . I think I'm gonna puke."

Desire

Time is a muddle. They haven't had enough sleep, their bodies are still in Belgium. Jake's eyes look lighter. Michel suppresses a giggle. They stagger down Broadway, holding each other up. What seemed yesterday like a threatening mass of dark-skinned strangers can now be clearly distinguished as thick-lipped Mexicans, expressionless blacks, mangy winos, ecstatic preachers, furtive hawkers peddling watches and jewelry, dancers, pimps, women, girls, women. In a movie theater, slumped over in seats that reek of Lysol, they both fall asleep, halfway through a movie that Jake was dying to see because of the title: *DESIRE!!!*

10

WHEN JAKE WAKES UP the first thing he sees, through half-closed eyelids, is Michel, working up a sweat in front of the mirror, kicking his leg in the stuffy room, twelve quick thrusts, his knee pulled up to his pelvis and his foot shooting out, each toe individually raised, at an invisible but deliberate target.

Michel takes a shower, trims his toenails on the lumpy sofa, whips out his *Hitlerjugend* dagger and polishes it with Kleenex and baby oil.

I'm sharing a room with a murderer, Jake thinks, and drinks the last gulp of beer out of the bottle next to his bed. It's still surprisingly fresh and frothy, even after a whole night. Belgian beer goes flat much quicker than American beer.

In a snack bar Jake bolts down a three-egg omelet and two side orders of hash browns.

"Where you from? You like it here?" asks the black girl who serves them. "Oh no, not again," mumbles Jake, and cries out, his mouth full of food, "Belgium. Very nice!"

Michel starts grumbling about a trio of bearded slobs who are sitting in the corner drinking milk. "Don't they have anything

better to do?" he mutters. "Look at their jeans, haven't been
washed in months, probably contaminating the whole place."

"Could be," says Jake.

That afternoon they set out for the Happiest Place on Earth,
an amusement park that originated in the brain of Walter Elias
Disney one Saturday afternoon as he and his two whiny daugh-
ters were sitting on a bench eating peanuts and he didn't know
what to do with the little brats, but as Jake and Michel go riding
through Los Angeles in a swaying hulk of a bus it gradually becomes clear to them, from the words of the tour guide, that
they've joined the wrong tour. For a moment they're afraid they'll
have to pay an obligatory visit to a crocodile farm, or that they'll
be hustled back into the Hollywood Bowl (which, as it so happens, has nothing to do with bowling in *our* country, you've got to
know your English pretty damn well before you can tell the difference between words like that!), but then, relieved, they march
along behind the other passengers through the gates of what is
certainly just as educational and worth telling the folks back
home, that is, Universal Studios, where Henry Kissinger once
spent a week, and Princess Margaret from England, and President Johnson's daughter Luci, it says so on a sign at the entrance.

They're driven around in a blood-red tram past hills and
forests and lakes and waterfalls and houses without rooms and
miniature castles from before World War I. Then they're hurried
into a mining car that zooms through a surging river, down a
mountainside, into a gorge whose walls split open and let loose
gigantic boulders that come crashing down toward them. Jake
screams at the top of his lungs and is immediately reprimanded
by a liveried guard for letting his arm hang overboard.

"It's just nerves," says Jake. "Beg your pardon, sir."

"Hey, that's okay!" the man blares into his microphone. "If your arm gets ripped off, we got plenty of spare parts!" Everyone howls with laughter.

The mining car races full speed over a shaky, weather-beaten bridge and makes it to the other side just in time, before the railings splinter, the bottom drops out, and the whole thing goes plunging into the waves.

"They mean well," says Jake. "It's supposed to be funny, but it's wasted on me." He wipes the clammy sweat from his face.

In a smooth brown lake a steely-gray triangle shoots up and cleaves the surface of the water, heading straight for a fisherman sitting resignedly in a rowboat. As the spectators cheer, the boat capsizes and the fisherman disappears in a rapidly reddening whirlpool. Then the gleaming back of a shark emerges and starts swimming toward Jake at breakneck speed. Five inches away from his ashen face the huge, gaping jaws rise from the water, with teeth like meat cleavers, and snap shut. Jake huddles against Michel, who pushes him back, roaring with laughter, toward the gnashing white teeth, the red-gray cavern of the mouth.

"I'm going home," says Jake.

But he's not allowed to leave the mining car, rules are rules. They ride sluggishly past rows of cannons, quaint little villages with elm trees and wooden churches. A stagecoach goes by, shots are fired from a church steeple, the horses rear, cowboys leap out of the stagecoach and gun down the bandit, who comes tumbling out of the belfry and lands with a thud in a pile of sand, identical streams of clear water shoot out of barrels, a faggot in a silver suit gets shot in the ass, hobbles off with one hand on his butt, and dives in through a splintering window.

A huge cliff appears, hung with icicles, the mining car climbs slowly to the top and plunges, screaming, into a ravine, screeches past the glittering walls of ice, shaking and wobbling, bitter-cold clouds lash our faces, we're frozen stiff, pine trees crackle, explode.

The cursed mining car goes lurching into a jungle, where dinosaurs rear up from a bed of quicksand, while ape-men are sucked down into its depths. From behind a shrub of green soap-suds a grizzly bear rises up and waves his paws in amazement. Past a row of poles topped with skulls, some of them three times as big as Didi's head. Emaciated wolf dogs bark in subterranean crypts at blustering buccaneers as they roll around in piles of gold and jewels, guarded by skeletons in frayed uniforms. Indians paddle by in canoes, spring a leak, drown. An orchestra of raccoons, foxes, and badgers plays "Puppy Love." Astronauts hop past craters, reach out shaky asbestos gloves, and plant American flags in a moonscape of pollen and ashes, while a children's choir sings a Christmas carol.

Then they're rushed out of the mining car, into the studios. Jake follows Michel, his knees like jelly. Jake hasn't heard a peep out of Michel the whole time. He's been walking around this colorful hell like he's back home on Veldstraat! The man's not human.

They shuffle along in serried ranks past the living rooms of Abraham Lincoln and Frank Sinatra, see a slide show about the making of *King Kong*, and are initiated into the art of illusion: how an ordinary human being can be transformed into a werewolf or a gnome, how it's impossible to film somebody licking an ice cream cone because the ice cream melts from the heat of the studio lamps—they usually use mashed potato instead.

In the souvenir shop at the exit Michel buys a thin rubber mask that's supposed to look like Frankenstein. He puts it on that night in their room.

"You're not going to walk around the street like that, are you?" asks Jake.

"Nah, it's for Markie. A present."

"What's he need it for?"

"I think it suits him. Don't you?"

"Markie's just a kid."

"Yes. That's what most people think," says Michel with an odd smile.

Once again they traipse, dog-tired, down the boulevard, past the brightly lit shop windows bulging with toys and radios, past the sinister-looking hotels. Just one more night and they're off to the City of Games, the Land of Glitter and Grit.

"What're you going to take back for Didi?" asks Michel in front of a shop window full of army fatigues.

"Got any ideas?"

"You're her father. You know best. You know *her.*"

Jake waits.

"You know her better than anyone," says Michel. "Or don't you?"

"Knowing isn't the same as healing," says Jake.

"It's the first step. Or isn't it?"

"Maybe."

"But then you've really got to know the person, down to the core."

"What're you trying to tell me? That she's not as sick as we say she is?"

"Hey, don't get so worked up."

"I guess I could buy her a paintbox," says Jake.

"Or one of those." Michel points to a white blouse with a lace collar and the words DO IT printed on the sleeves in saffron-yellow letters. "You could have your name printed on it. Jake. Or Papa. Or your picture."

"The picture in my passport?"

"Any picture you want. Or a picture of somebody else. Markie, for instance."

What does he mean by that? Michel never just says something, there's always more to it. Jake is about to demand an explanation when a police car with a shrieking siren pulls up at the curb, right alongside them. The siren keeps wailing as two cops in sunglasses, one fat and one thin, pounce on a young man in dingy white jeans. They yank at his arms and push him around. After a while the fat cop grabs him by the collar and flings him against the car. The youth bends over without a whimper and flattens his hands against the car window. The cop kicks apart his calves and frisks him, his fingers moving like fat, wriggling worms along his ears, his crotch, his boots. Giggling, the cop straightens up.

"Come on," says Jake. "Let's go," he says to Michel, who can't take his eyes off this little scene.

"What for?" he asks, lighting a cigarette.

"You look much too much like those Ethiopians they got around here."

Michel runs his hand over his hip, feeling for his dagger. The slant of light from a shop window accentuates his full lips, his kinky hair.

The cops put their heads together. Then the fat one pulls the kid off the car by his belt and gives him a casual kick in the rear. The youth mumbles something and walks away, his shoulders hunched. Just as the cops are about to get back into their car, they see Michel. As if Michel, with that insolent bearing of his, that sardonic sneer on the half-breed lips curled around the unlit cigarette, has willed them to notice him. They stare; lights from the passing cars flash in their jet-black lenses.

"Hey, you," says the fat cop.

"Who, me?" says Michel, unperturbed.

"Yeah, you," says the skinny cop. "Aren't you Vinnie Siralomo's kid brother?"

"Yeah," says Michel. "What about it?" His cigarette stays perfectly level.

"You better watch your ass," says the beanpole, and turns his unprotected, vulnerable back to Michel. Reluctantly, the fat cop climbs into the car, too. Then slowly, with a fearful wailing, the car glides away.

"Vinnie's brother, he says!"

"If Vinnie hears that, honey, you're dead."

"He'll rip out your liver, dollface."

"You're cat food, Tweetie-Pie!"

Lazy, mocking voices behind them. Where are they coming from? Jake and Michel watch as a dozen youths emerge from doorways, saunter over to their motorcycles, and lean against them in a semicircle. Two of the youths stand arm in arm, like a bride and groom posing for a photograph. Nearly all are dressed in dark leather, with medals and logo patches on their jackets. Black leather gloves. Lots of dyed hair, clipped short. Lipstick. Silver dollar earrings. Glittering eyes, moist lips. Pimples, scars. Skintight pants stretched over well-padded flies. Sensual, drawling voices.

"Should we go get Vinnie?"

"He's dining at Ma Maison, darling."

"Tell him his brother's lookin' for him."

They coo like doting old ladies, poking each other in the ribs. One of them, a kid who can't be more than twelve, thumps himself on the belly and gives a piercing cry. "Oh dear, oh dear!" Or was it *"O dio, o dio"*?

And then a dark, hoarse, whiskey-worn voice says:

"Leave 'em alone." (A distant echo of the long-suffering, confident tone Jake adopts when he intervenes in a brawl at the Unicorn.) "Leave those cocksuckers alone." A drab-looking broad with square shoulders wrapped in an army blanket is standing next to one of the motorcycles, stroking the seat with a chapped hand. She's wearing at least five pairs of woollen socks and three baggy sweaters full of holes. Around her neck is a dog collar with brass studs. Her sweaty, battered face is painted in various pastel tints (yes, as if Didi has colored her in with the whole box of crayons).

The leather-clad ephebi cheer. *Aryans*, it says on the back of their jackets.

"Oooh, Mama Rachel is hot for the fat guy!"

"Oooh, Rachel and the fat guy!"

"Two fuckin' Landrovers!" They all start making crackling, sputtering sounds, their cheeks puffed out like balloons. No, not all of them. Jake sees that there is one among them who doesn't take part in this foolish, lustful taunting. He's sitting sideways on his bike, slightly older than the rest, with shaved eyebrows. That's their leader, Jake decides, and strides up to him, two Flemish giant steps.

"Excuse me, is that your wife?" asks Jake, pointing to the sixty-year-old alley cat, who laughs incredulously, with pearly white teeth that, apart from the whites of her eyes, are her only unblemished features.

The leader doesn't understand Jake, or doesn't want to understand him, he just stares. Next to him a motorcycle revs up, threateningly; the exhaust pipe rattles.

The whelps close their circle, yelping and squeaking.

"He wants to marry Rachel!"

"He's *got* to marry Rachel, she's having his baby!"

"Can you ride one of these things?" asks the leader. His voice is nearly as light as Jake's, slightly hoarser. He points to the largest bike, which is hung with metal ornaments, troll dolls, and pennants, one of them with the fiery letters ARYANS.

Jake nods. Michel comes over and stands next to him and says, "Me, too."

"I didn't ask you," says the leader, without looking at him.

He has a smooth, lofty forehead, his reddish hair is slicked back with gel, his eyebrows are two identical arcs of black nylon thread.

"Where're you from, sweetheart?"

"Belgium," says Jake.

"Where's that? In Europe?"

The broad-shouldered rag lady wriggles her way through the circle, bores her clear eyes fringed with purple and green false lashes into Jake's. "Tell him, baby," she laughs.

"In Europe," says Jake.

She touches him, a flutter of aging fingers, just below the navel.

"Belgium's a sweet country," she says. "*You're* sweet." Which unleashes a caterwaul of meowing and braying from the bikers.

"Hey, fatty, you a communist?" one of them asks.

"Tell him, baby," says Rachel, stroking Jake's belly.

"All Europeans are communists, or at least they will be," says the leader. Jake takes a deep breath. He's hungry. Just nerves.

In the distance, the police siren wails.

The leader tosses his followers a casual glance, then flings one leg over his bike. Straddling the great metal beast, he raises his hand and thrusts his black leather palm in Jake's direction.

"Go without fear," he says. "And may the Force be with you," and the howling pack falls silent, Rachel too, and allows them to pass, and they dash across the street, right in front of the police car as it glides steadily closer, weeping and wailing.

‖ ‖

SURROUNDED BY SHAGGY WAR VETS with tattooed biceps, Michel shoots down elk, bison, yellow ducks that shatter to bits in the cardboard sky with a venomous jingling of bells, and then something goes wrong and he misses every next shot, a volley of ducks goes clattering through the air, elk and bison roll past the hesitant barrel of his gun. Jake is just wondering whether the veterans might have made Michel nervous, whether Michel is afraid they might challenge him, when he notices that the word MARKSMAN has flashed onto the scoreboard.

"Markie's our man," says Jake.

"Yup, seems like he's everywhere," says Michel, and strolls, more indifferently than ever, out of the shooting gallery.

The pavement is warm, chewing gum sticks to the soles of their shoes.

Jake eats three soggy rolls with pastrami and mustard. At the entrance to the club, where Michel buys tickets, he treats himself to two chocolate bars and a creamsicle. The club is half full. A giggly, inordinately bowing black man escorts them, waving his flashlight and whispering, "This way, brothers," until, squeezing their way past chairs and legs, they find themselves in a dark alcove. On a stage that divides the club down the middle, in the white cone of a spotlight, a nude dancer is twisting her generous curves into impossible contortions. The air smells of wet hay. The waiter sets four whiskeys down on their table.

"That's so they don't have to bother us if we want another drink during the show," says Jake. "They've got real good manners here in America." When his eyes get used to the light he sees the other spectators, most of them in workaday clothes, gaping, motionless, at the creamy, rippling belly of the dancer as it quivers and shakes. He imagines that Rachel must've had a belly like that once, not so very long ago. The three-piece band spurs her on. The woman squats down, swings her bountiful breasts, prances around the stage, spreads her thighs amid stifled cheers from several members of the audience, and sinks back. The spotlight follows her. Then she whips open her legs and drums them against the wooden floor, kicking up a cloud of dust. For a moment Jake thinks she's having a fit, because the raucous gargling sounds coming out of her mouth as her heels tap furiously against the ground remind him of the falling sickness, but that can't be true, because Michel, who's something of a doctor himself, is smiling and winking at him.

"Look," says Michel. "Over there." Three men in Hawaiian shirts at a table in front of them are laughing differently, moving and whispering differently, than the rest of the audience. Lewd, awkward, defiant—they must be Belgian.

"Yes," says Jake.

The dancer claws with rough, spatulate fingers (that remind Jake of Rachel's chapped hands) at her sumptuous breasts, twiddles her nipples between thumb and forefinger like the knobs on a radio, licks a nipple with her eyes crossed.

"Mmmm, yummy," she says.

Then she sinks back again, supporting herself on her palms and her heels in the silver sandals, her knees part, the thin ribbon between her thighs glistens and dances like an aluminum adder. Her belly seethes.

"You should never do that after eating," says Jake.

Michel doesn't answer, he's staring at the backs of those three Belgian necks.

A roll of the kettle drums and the dancer drops dead in a cloud of pale, wriggling dust motes. This is met with a smattering of applause.

"And that, boys, was our charming guest from Denver, Colorado, Miss Mammy Malone!" Clapping her hands, a slight, heavily powdered woman in a grass-green tuxedo with a mousseline jabot springs into view and grabs hold of the microphone.

"Mammy," says Jake approvingly. "Good name for her. Hey, what's wrong?" he asks worriedly. "Can't you see? Are we too far away?"

"Not far enough," says Michel. "I'm fed up to the balls with this."

"Aha!" cries the lady in the tux. "I see we've got company!" She goes to the edge of the stage and looks Jake straight in the eye. "And they're connoisseurs of womanly beauty, you can tell! Especially the big guy, the fat one. Isn't that right, big boy?"

Jake nods, bright red, and gulps down his whiskey.

"My name's Violet," she says. "What's yours?"

Jake's swollen face, the bulging eyes, the pale lashes, turns to Michel.

"She means you," he says.

"Oh, our friend here is incognito!" cries the green scrag. "Could he be a diplomat from one of the many, *too* many United Nations?"

The audience, snickering, turns to Jake with a look of expectation, mockery, and hate. Jake sinks lower and lower in his chair and tries to hide behind the restless, fleshy backs of the Belgians; it's no use. He slips down off his chair and starts hunting around under the table for a cigarette he supposedly dropped. When he hears the malicious, rattling laugh above him that can only be Michel, he makes ready to duck-walk his way to the exit.

"Hey, where'd you go, Mr. Diplomat?" The laughter in the room grows louder. Jake surfaces, his heart pounding, and drinks his second whiskey in one gulp.

"You're not scared of me, are you, my chubby darling?" cries the shrill voice.

"What's there to be scared of? This?" In one fluid motion she unbuttons her dinner jacket and starts kneading her pear-shaped, girlish breasts. Her nipples are painted ruby-red.

"Stupid goat!" Jake swears in a high-pitched mumble. The music starts up, a sultry, teasing lament.

"Hey, Violet, take it off!" shouts one of the Belgians, in Flemish. She gives a sign to the band, which immediately stops playing, and peers into the audience, her hands on her hips.

"What'd you say?"

"Take it off!" blusters the Belgian. Suddenly there's something nervous, alert, about Michel. Jake notices how he removes his elbows from the table, straightens up in his chair.

"What's that you're speaking? Australian?" asks Violet with a crooked, humble smile.

"Flemish! What else?" shouts the Belgian, and his friends chime in, "Flemish, goddamit!"

"Hey, seriously, where're you boys from? I can't understand a word you're saying." Violet has turned into a slightly exasperated schoolmistress.

"From Kruishoutem!"

"Where they've got the best eggs in Europe!"

"And the best studs!"

They switch to English.

"Eggs!"

"Best eggs in the country! My town!"

Saxophone. The dry tapping of the lightest stick against the lightest drumhead. Electric guitar chords.

"Okay, boys," says Violet, laughing. "Grab hold of your eggs and *scramble* 'em!" She unzips both sides of her pants, tosses the grass-green panels onto a chair, then her jacket, then the jabot. She stands there, stark naked, with a rounded white belly and evenly trimmed bronze-colored pubic hair, the exact same color as her sculpted curls.

"It's a wig," says Michel. "See?"

"Top or bottom?"

"Bottom."

Could be. Michel knows about these things. Fascinated, Jake stares at the close-clipped tussock, wishing he could peel it right off. But what would he find? A childlike slit. He refuses to think any more about it and is busy concentrating on Violet's jaunty yet wooden movements, her lolling tongue, her quivering belly, when Michel gets up from his chair.

"I'm leaving."

"Why?"

"I've seen enough."

"Why?"

"You can stay if you want."

"No," says Jake. "I wouldn't do that."

"Then let's go."

Cursing, Jake steps out from behind the table, amid hissing

and grunting from the audience. As they walk past the spotlight their shadows slant across Violet, who is marching in place like a miniature soldier, knees high in the air. Wiglet.

In front of the thick curtains at the exit, the giggly black man asks if there's anything else he can do for them. Michel glances quickly at Jake.

"Go lift a leg," says Michel.

"Okay," says Jake. "Where?"

The black man points the way. Just as Jake is closing the door, he sees him bending slavishly toward Michel, awaiting his instructions.

Michel takes out his fountain pen and scribbles on the back of a coaster: "Bastard, don't think I didn't see you last year at the Stud Society Ball in Kruishoutem! My punishment shall be terrible! Rickabone."

Jake comes back just in time to see Michel handing the coaster and a ten-dollar bill to the eagerly nodding nigger and pointing out the three unsuspecting Belgians.

12

THE NEXT MORNING STARTS OUT ALL WRONG. The concierge won't reserve seats for them on the bus to Las Vegas. The bank around the corner refuses to change their Belgian money because they don't have an account there. Bank tellers in America are all a bunch of crooks! There isn't a single cab, because the biggest taxi firm went bankrupt three days ago.

They lug their bulky suitcases through the sunbaked streets to the bus station. They're sick to death of this city, which may be fine for tourists who like going to museums full of dinosaur bones, or frying their brains on a Pacific beach, or being ripped off by the male and female scum you see for sale on every street corner, but which, for two Knights of the Unicorn, can be nothing more than a delay en route to the City of Chance.

Should they buy a round-trip ticket?

"Of course not," says Michel. "With all the money we're gonna win, we're *flying* back!"

Standing outside the bus station, where they have to wait a quarter of an hour—too short to hit a bar, but too long to go dry—is a helmeted youth with a shuddering Yamaha 250 cc between his knees.

96

"If only we were younger," sighs Jake, "We'd knock him cold and zoom off on his bike."

"It has nothing to do with being young."

"You're right," says Jake. "It's 'cause we had such a good upbringing."

A blond girl rips up a letter and flings it into a garbage can, walks away, comes back a moment later, digs the strips of paper out of the garbage, reads a few lines, and tears them into postage stamps. The tiny squares flutter into the gutter.

Jake and Michel sit down at the back of the bus (you can smoke in the last two rows). The bus is cool and half-empty.

Hours go by and there's nothing to see. Any other tourist would be thrilled, pointing ecstatically at the view, the Mohave Desert, the cactuses, the sun glinting off the mountaintops, just like in a cowboy movie, but Jake and Michel thumb through *Penthouse* and *Playboy* (which they're planning to take back with them to the Unicorn, because in Belgium you can get magazines like these but only in mutilated condition; somewhere in a suburb of Brussels, by order of the ministry, special clerks spend all day in fluorescent-lit basements going through huge stacks of magazines and sponging out every prick and cunt with a wad of cotton dipped in acetone).

Jake is busy studying a soft-focus shot of a redhaired goddess ripping off her lace panties with one hand and playing her labia like piano keys with the other, when a deep, cheerful voice behind him says: "Not bad, not bad at all."

A black woman in a white pantsuit is smiling at him. She has wide-set eyes, like a sheep, or Jackie Kennedy, and she's either drunk or happy or stupid because she winks at Jake like he's an old friend.

"Hey, brother," she says to Michel, who winces. "You two on vacation?"

97

"No," says Jake, quickly closing his *Penthouse*. "We're on our way to make money."

"Oowhee!" crows the black lady. "Vegas, here we come!" She puts her silver-ringed hand on Michel's shoulder, heaves herself up, and plops down in the seat next to him, right on top of all his other magazines full of spread-eagled women.

"I'm on vacation. My first day. Life's a party!"

Michel agrees, in silence.

"And I'm gonna have me a good time. Oh, yeah, you bet I am. How 'bout you? You like havin' a good time? Where're you stayin' in Vegas?"

"Don't know yet."

"Great. Me neither. You gonna have a good time in Vegas?"

"You bet," says Michel.

"That's my boy!" she shouts, squeezing his thigh. "You think I'm pretty?"

Michel nods. He looks miserable, but Jake knows him well enough by now to know that it's a facade, a ploy, a defense.

"You mean it?"

"Sure."

"Then you're in good company, 'cause Dean Martin told me the same thing. Laurie, he said, ain't no one prettier 'n you." Her head nods, her bloodshot eyes fall closed. "Ridin' on a bus always makes me horny. How 'bout you?"

"Not really," says Michel.

"You're kiddin'!" The drowsy eyes open.

"No."

She rocks back and forth in her seat and nuzzles her woozy face against Michel's neck. He pushes her away. "Oh, how very bitter, my sweet!" she sings, at the top of her lungs.

"She likes you," Jake whispers. "I think you've got a chance!"

"What'd he say? C'mon, honey, tell me, what'd he say?"

"That I've got a chance."

"What chance?" she asks, her face puckered into a frown. "You ain't got a chance in the world. Not you, not me, not nobody!" she screams at the other passengers. One of them, an old man in a black silk skullcap with two round black Mickey Mouse ears, turns around and says, "Right on, lady!"

"Right on!" she shouts back gaily, and grabbing Michel's hand, she traces the lines in his palm with a varnished fingernail. "Oooh, honey, you wouldn't believe all the poontang you're gonna get in Vegas. You like to fuck, baby?"

"You?" Michel shoots back.

"I asked first, baby. Do you?" She tickles his palm.

"Sure."

She gets up. Resolutely, almost gruffly, she grabs Michel's arm with both hands and tugs, hard. "C'mon, I can't wait."

Michel wrenches his arm away. "Sorry."

"Whaddya mean, Sorry, darlin'? Do you want to or don't you?"

"Oh, yes," says Jake, snorting and swearing with delight. "Sonofabitch, yes, darling!"

"No thanks," says Michel.

She leans on his armrest, sways back and forth, staggers to the last row, falls against the door of the restroom, and bellows, "Get over here, you bastard!"

Michel turns white as a sheet. Blindly, he snatches the *Penthouse* out of Jake's hands, bangs it open, stares. The bus rides through a rust-brown plain; the rivers are empty and dry. Sunlight spangles the corrugated metal roofs of the sheepfolds where the Indians live. They sit inside among gunnysacks full of corn-meal and crates of chickens, playing poker and drinking some-thing distilled from cactuses. The air in the bus rustles, cool, thin.

The black lady comes back and swings her handbag against Michel's averted shoulder. "I love you, you nasty man," she says. "C'mon." Michel stays where he is; any minute now he's going to explode. The black lady kneels down and absently picks bits of lint off his sleeve.

"My Mama used to say, 'Laurie, you go out there and take what you want. Before it's too late. 'Cause before you know it you'll be as old as me.' "

"Why don't you take *him?*" says Michel.

"Are you crazy?" hisses Jake. "Shut up!"

"No," says the black lady gravely. "*You're* the one, little brother. You're jus' my size, I can tell. C'mon. Quit whinin'." Once again she heads off to the restroom, singing "I Get a Kick Out of You," but the song ends in babbling and muttering. She's in there fif-teen, twenty minutes, probably fallen asleep, or maybe even died, with the fatal needle sticking up out of her thigh. A lady in Bermudas pulls open the door of the restroom, gasps, and asks worriedly, "Are you all right, miss?" The whole bus hears her bestial roar, "You get that bastard over here, sugar!"

"Are you ill?" asks the lady.

"Yes! Yes! Yes!" The bus watches as the reckless lady disappears into the doorway . . . only to go shooting out again two seconds later like a human cannonball and flying against the aluminum wall of the bus. "My God!" pants the lady. The deep, cheerful, black voice moans, "C'mon back, sugar. C'mon. I'll be real nice to you. We'll have fun, darlin'. Men are no damn good, when you get right down to it."

The lady bustles indignantly up the aisle to the driver. He

scratches the back of his neck as she makes her complaint, but the bus doesn't slow down, doesn't stop. Furious, on the verge of tears, the lady stumbles back to her seat.

In the middle of the desert two bony white greyhounds go spurting past. Any other traveler would know why. What kind of desert animals, what plants or grasses they eat. Whether they've escaped from a traveling circus. Or maybe they're training for a dog race.

Jake reaches under his seat and pulls out a white high-heeled shoe with a purple strap.

"Take it home for Dina," says Michel.

"No. She may have big feet, but this is a submarine!"

"So give it back."

"Back?"

Michel nods toward the rear of the bus. Jake immediately flings the shoe to the ground. A few minutes later he picks it up again and puts it in his lap, turns it around and around, examines the trodden-down soles, the scuffed heel.

"It's kind of sad," he says. "The first day of your vacation, crying your eyes out on a traveling toilet seat—"

"She's not crying her eyes out."

"Oh, yes she is."

"Then go cheer her up."

"That'd be the right thing to do, I guess. But she can't help it, you know."

"All the more reason to help *her.*"

"Why don't *you* go?"

"Me? I'd probably end up kicking her," says Michel brightly.

"I know that," says Jake.

"Well?"

"Well, what?"

"Are you going or aren't you?"

"I would, if only to make her feel better, but I haven't got the nerve. Don't want to give her any ideas, you know what I mean? And besides, I can't get all mixed up with just anybody who happens to be unhappy."

"She's not just anybody. She's the only one who needs you. One single person. In the whole United States of America. Is that too much to ask?"

"It scares me."

"Then shut the hell up about how sad it is."

Fifteen minutes later the black lady comes back, gurgling and hawking up another song, and nudges Michel. "Hey, I'm talkin' to you. Yeah, you. I've been waitin' for you the whole time. You promised. We were gonna have fun. Hey, what's the matter, you don't wanna talk to a nigger? Hey! You rather sit and flirt with Fatso here? Hey! Don' think I didn't have you pegged the minute I saw you, oh yes, you two are from the sentimental brigade! I spotted you right off, baby!" With a decisive yet indifferent gesture, she tosses a cottony white rag flecked with blood into Michel's lap. Hissing like a mountain cat, he spreads his legs, but the filthy thing sticks to his thigh. He sweeps it away with his *Penthouse*. She roars with laughter, flashing her wide, pink tongue.

"I'll knock your teeth out!" shouts Michel.

She stretches her thick lips, the lips that look like Michel's, as wide as she can, holds on to her side, and stammers out, "Oh yeah? Is that what you wanna do? Really truly, darlin'? Laurie would like nuthin' better. Go ahead!"

Her face suddenly crumples, deep furrows appear along her nostrils and the corners of her mouth. "Even that's too much for you, faggot." She heaves a dry sob, gasps for breath, and sinks back down into her seat, singing, praying, drooling. "My Mama told me when I left home, 'Laurie, you go out there and take what you want, baby,' and I said, 'I'll show 'em, Mama, all those bastards down in Vegas, they're gonna stand up and take notice when Laurie comes walkin' in, you bet they are, 'cause Dean Martin kissed my pussy, don't you forget it, Dean Martin said, 'Laurie, my fine slut,' and he wasn't drunk neither, don't you forget it."

When the bus pulls into Barstow, the last stop before Las Vegas, and Jake and Michel step out with the rest of the passengers, stiff-legged and dazed, into the hot, stuffy afternoon, the woman stays behind in her seat, rigid, asleep with her eyes open.

Jake and Michel drink Anchor Steam, the beer drinker's beer—rich, creamy head, deep amber color, a kiss of hops—in a bar that's furnished like a ship's saloon, surrounded by men in garishly checked cotton suits who shake hands with the barkeeper-in-captain's-hat, begging, "Wish us luck, Bill!" and he does, grinning at so much faith and hope.

Fifteen minutes later a Cadillac with a dying siren pulls up alongside the bus. Two policemen climb into the bus and escort the black lady to their car. She doesn't protest, just hands over her bag, which they immediately search. Then, limping on one white shoe, she does a drunken jig in front of the hood and sings, "Oh, What a Beautiful Morning!" until one of the cops shoves her into the car. They zoom off in a cloud of dust that settles over a rack of miniature slot machines outside the bar. Souvenirs.

From Barstow to Las Vegas the desert is one long, empty stretch. But then poles with billboards rise up against the backdrop of Prussian blue mountains, more and more and closer and closer together, with neon lights telling you where you can get married in half an hour, where you can play poker and craps and 25,000-dollar keno with a free buffet lunch, where nude Swedish girls (no kidding!) will give you a full body massage, where you can buy red-hot hot dogs, where you can consult the Savior twenty-four hours a day.

"We've still got an hour to go and they're already trying to brainwash us," says Jake, who reads all the ads out loud, faster and faster.

The sky turns orange and turquoise, just like on the postcards. In the shreds of desert that go flashing by they see brave men hunting for scorpions to press into plastic cubes. Look great on your desk, real eye-catchers. Female scorpions are sold to pharmacists, for their venom.

Then at last, on the horizon, a hazy streak of light, like the immeasurably vast cloud above a fire, that heralds the Neon City, and for the first time Michel laughs, weary, yet eager as a boy.

13

—THE THIRD DAY NOW, or is it the fourth? day and night run together in the merciless light, as they sometimes do in that land far away, in our town, now and then, in the Unicorn, when things are really moving in the game and nobody's willing to give up their cards, even if it takes all night and all day, but here it seems, when I take a good look around me, which I can't always because I'm staring so hard at the roulette ball, the baccarat cards, or the dice, here it seems *normal*, the trembling sun outside and the light inside, however muted, is blinding, sometimes the light feels like air, as if we're being lit up inside and out, the nights are short and flushed with light, we'll fall asleep for a couple of hours with our clothes on, in bed or on the sofa, but then the light shines right through to our glands and one of us—usually Michel—wakes with a start and then the other—me—why, oh why?—has to go with him when he dashes off to the gaming tables like a blinded hare that knows it'll end up in the beams of a jacklight or under a Cadillac but wants one last chance to dance, hiccuping and hopping, in a garden of neon, a park of shimmering light, a world of violence and secrets—

(Jake is sitting in his boxer shorts at the dressing table in the

motel room. On the cigarette-proof Formica tabletop that's supposed to pass for cherry wood lies a piece of airmail stationery.
He sucks on a ball point, his toes curl in the orange nylon carpet
full of cigarette holes, the city hums and the pool filters roar.)

—the third day now and I'm still not all here, still feeling kind
of shaky, but I'm getting used to it, even though I'm not quite
myself yet, Michel told me just now, two hours ago, that he was
going to the whores, don't believe it for a minute, he only said it
for appearance's sake because after three whole days a man like
him is expected to shoot his wad—

—I should really write to Dina, a second letter, not as whiny as
the first, not about her or us or Desire but about the desert for instance, about the danger, about being a stranger, but when'll I
find the time? I'd have plenty of time if I wasn't always chasing after *him*, after that half-crazed greyhound that races from one
gaming table to the next, sometimes you think he'll stop for a
while at the Texas hold-'em table, not my kind of game, give me
five-card stud any day, but before you know it he's on to the next,
'cause either the dealer's been giving him funny looks or he's
playing against him, and only him, or else it's me who's getting in
his way because I'm playing at the same table, but if I'm not
around and if I'm standing at the roulette table, it makes him even
more nervous, he says, 'cause I am his responsibility after all and
he'd rather be able to keep an eye on me, and you can't play like
that, you've got to let yourself go, like floating on your back in a
swimming pool, mellow, as they say around here, then maybe
you've got a chance—

—now would be a good time to write a letter, my left leg's
asleep, but what's there to write? "Dearest Dina, dearest Didi,"
no, I'd rather save it all for when I get home, that first night back
in my plush armchair, a nice cold Trappist in my hand, by the

time I get through telling them about the trip they'll think they were here themselves. They should be here. Dina, anyway. She'd never believe her eyes, that vixen of mine, my heartbeat, she'd never show it, of course, she'd go strutting around with her nose in the air like she was born and bred here in Vegas, like she's seen it all a thousand times before on TV, but if she could see me now—just once—she wouldn't recognize me because a person breathes differently here, moves differently, just look at all the others, at the Americans, even they move differently than back home—me, for instance, I walk much more lightly and easily and briskly like I'm walking on air and no, sir, it's not just because of those basketball shoes I bought around the corner, it's the *light*—

—wonder how much weight I've lost, how much lighter I am? Ten pounds, at least. I gulp down my food because it tastes so bad, no wonder the young people around here are covered with pimples, mashed cardboard hamburgers every day of the week—

—I won't sleep a wink, again, mostly because I'll be waiting up for him even though he explicitly, expressly told me: "Go to sleep." I better get a hold of myself or next thing you know I'll be on my way to Westward Ho! to mark a bunch of keno tickets to give to one of those coolly smiling princesses in their fishnet stockings, they smile like they mean it but aren't allowed to, Thank you, sir, good luck, a person should have at least one chance in his life, not only with those well-trained, frosty robots, but at keno, I mean, with twenty numbers out of eighty you should have, *must* have, at least one . . . Must? Yes, must, if, if, supposing, should, would've won, if, yes, and if my aunt had balls she'd be my uncle—

—I've eaten up all the Bountys, Mars bars, Milk Duds, Cheese Doodles, marshmallows, I'm still starving—

—if I stretch my neck I can just see the dented cowboy hat with the brim sticking out above the roof of the Flamingo, a wavy line of neon light, wonder what it costs per second, all that light—

—soon, but not soon enough: daylight. Then pancakes, with syrup and sausages, I'm starving—

—what's he doing now? Gone off with one of those seventeen-year-olds who sit and leer at you from a dark corner of the bar, pepped to the gills? No, His Lordship is sitting, at ease in his un-ease, at the card table, scraping a card softly, impatiently, on the felt, and begging, pleading: "Lord, have mercy, give me a nice, round, decisive, annihilating three, help me, O Lord, to destroy our mutual enemy, this damnable dealer, cross-eyed with greed," and he gets dealt his card, frowns, pushes back his chair, he's been burned once too many, and he peers over the shoulders of the other players at the treacherous keno board, and goes to the craps table, but he doesn't play, craps is too common, too loud, all those crazy Appalachian hillbillies kissing their dice before they throw 'em, rubbing the tits of their hillbilly wives and whooping and hollering, no, he, Michel, never redeemed, forever playing, has to do it in secret, in silent, marshy solitude, that's how he plays with people, too, pulling their strings in the darkness to see what'll come gushing out of those quivering marionettes—

—people in Las Vegas are much fatter than in Los Angeles—

—sometimes he looks at me like I'm some nasty, stubborn dealer—

—you never see people like that back home, that girl with the silver wires around her teeth who yelled like Tarzan when she caught the jingling wave of coins, the Indian in his pajamas, that idiot walking around with an arrow through his head, two halves of a rubber arrow above his ears, he must've been pretty far gone, and what about that bus full of loonies in white rabbit ears, and those shady-looking young Mexicans in polyester jackets, the old man in shorts with paper-white knees and a bloody eye, you never see that back home, Thank God, you might say, but why? Maybe the whole world should be this way, no worrying about what other people think, no bitching, beefing, bellyaching, just doing whatever you like, just *feeling*, delicious rage or pleasure or sorrow about something that happens right under your nose, here it's desire, the yearning for, for, for that one card that doesn't turn up for so agonizingly long, your favorite card, for me it's the queen of clubs, for Michel, who's much more logical, it's the eight of hearts, one of those cards halfway between ace and deuce, and why hearts? because of the bloodthirsty, plastic, scarlet desire he's so good at hiding, that Michel—

—the Flamingo, the Sahara, where the waiters look like bleached Bedouins, Caesar's Palace, with those statues of emperors right out of a wax museum giving you a *heil*-Hitler salute and the girls dressed in togas so short they barely cover their bronzed or are they shiny brown spray-painted butts, epaulettes on their shoulders like World War I generals, the Pioneer, with cowboys in all shapes and sizes, the Dunes, no, Dina, I'll take Circus Circus any day—

—not that we're so bad off in our motel, it's the biggest motel on earth, there are thousands of rooms and forty pools, it takes fifteen minutes to walk from the reception desk to your door, past the stark-lit stucco walls, the whirring metal cases full of Pepsi and Sprite cans—

—but best of all, Dina, and it really gave me a fright the first time I saw it, is Circus Circus, where you're sitting there playing and suddenly the spotlights go on and in the middle of hundreds of rattling slot machines you hear a golden voice, you can't understand the names the voice is calling out, but it makes you all hot and restless, and then *they* appear, on all the ladders at once, silver acrobats, so glitteringly alike you can't tell if they're men or women or neither, they march around the ring, they climb the ladders in time to the music, up and down, they laugh and wave without even seeing us, that's how absorbed they are in their own angelic game, every movement is perfectly timed, like they're from some other planet, they hang, stretch, tumble, and climb up to the rafters, where they disappear, they go shooting into heaven, and my heart stood still, Dina, I was gasping for breath. "What the hell are you dreaming about?" said Michel.

(and Jake falls asleep, his hot cheek against his forearm, and basks in the thrilling, chilling vision shot through with rising and falling rainbow-colored fountains. Saliva dribbles from his mouth, he mumbles in his sleep, "I never want to leave here." The golden voice answers amid tambourines and lyres and the braying of slave girls, camels, and mules: "Fear not, I shall protect you wherever you go, and I shall bring you back to your land, and to Didi.")

14

"**Blackjack, that's my game,**" says Michel (my destiny, my calling . . . at last, a maneuver in which I can detect and exploit the enemy's flaw, his moment of weakness, so that he, in his isolation behind the table, goes rigid with shame).

"Are you calling it quits?" asks Jake.

"For today, anyway. For tonight, at least."

"How'd you make out? Did you win?"

"Six hundred bucks. Three blackjacks in a row."

"Which table?"

"That one." Michel looks triumphantly at a dealer across the room.

"He was tired," says Michel. "The last half hour he hadn't had any customers. He wanted to go home, but the pit boss had his eye on him. He was having doubts, I could tell, I stood four times on seventeen. I should probably go on playing." (Give in to that itching, eager, bittersweet surge of desire, adrenaline, vertigo.) "But I think I'll wait and get him the next time."

Jake calls it quits too. He throws one last time, with a sidelong flick of the wrist, like he's putting a spin on a Ping-Pong ball. A three. The yellow-powdered black lady next to him fingers the cross around her withered neck and shakes the dice.

"There's an eleven in there," says Jake, turning away. "I don't want to look. Come on."

"I'm paying," says Michel. They walk past the sloping, mirrored walls, which multiply the crystal chandeliers and rattling slot machines tenfold, to the exit, where there's less of a din and they can hear the sound of a piano being tuned. Didi playing. Jake stops in his tracks.

"I've got to mail another postcard before morning," he says. "Don't let me forget."

Outside, in the blistering light, Michel pounds his fist against the slot machine that's supposed to sell newspapers. He jerks at the handle, but the coin slot is jammed.

"Damn thing's always broken," says a passerby, a local in a creased white suit. "Whaddya want, the latest news?"

"The addresses of the restaurants and shows," Michel pants out as he fiddles with the padlock.

"What kinda shows? Dirty, real dirty?"

Jake nods vigorously.

"Bottoms Up," says the man. "That's where they show the most cunt. But if it's something really classy you want, really artistic, you should go to Guys and Dolls."

"Thanks."

The man follows them. He takes out a piece of jewelry, they can have it for half price, it's a genuine turquoise mounted in genuine silver by a genuine, pure-blooded Zuni Indian.

"Fuck off," says Michel cheerfully.

"The hottest chicks, the ones who'll do anything you want, you can beat 'em black and blue if you like, are at the Chicken Ranch," says the man. "I'll take you there myself, free of charge, half an hour's drive. Where're you guys from? Belgium? Man, I had the time of my life in Brussels, Chez Martine, the hottest chicks . . ." He's still talking to them, to their window, as the taxi drives off.

Michel treats them to dinner at the Jolly Trolley, six and a half dollars for a king-size steak. You can choose it yourself from the plastic-wrapped hunks of meat next to the grill.

Bottoms Up doesn't look very promising, the pictures outside the entrance are yellowed and the guy at the door comes on a little too strong, so they duck into a boisterous club across the street, the Valley of Dolls.

To Michel's annoyance, the dolls talk to the audience while they're dancing. He finds it distracting, he didn't come here to get to know the bitches, he doesn't want to be reminded of who they are, all he wants is to see the slowly unpeeled cunt that you, in the hollow egg of silence at the center of that frenzied music, can transform, enlarge, make wetter, wider, redder, fleshier, until it slurps you up, kinky hair, ears, thick lips, and all. The quasi-lascivious prattle, the seductive throat, the lisping, that's for other people, in hotel rooms, not for Michel, who undergoes it like a short circuit in the electrically charged, darkened rooms of his brain. The strobe light. The albino acting as master of ceremonies, market vendor, clown. The full, low-slung buttocks of a Negress. A fifty-year-old slut dressed as a schoolgirl, with fake braids and white knee socks. A frisky Filipina waggling a whip.

"This one's not bad," whispers Jake. She's tall, ash-blond, with flaccid cheeks and a wondrous gaze, gray, myopic eyes with bilious green lids, and thick, fluttering lashes.

"Hi there," she says to Jake. "What's your name?"

"Jake."

"Hi, Jack, my name's Leah." She laughs, flashing her wet, pink tongue and palate. Do they paint themselves on the inside, too? Pink toothpaste?

"Leah!" cries the albino. "A simple girl from a Quaker family from Haran who, at the tender age of eleven, was national banjo champion!"

Leah glides forward. Without taking her eyes off Jake she strokes the inside of her thighs and, with a curved, lacquered index fingernail, starts twanging furiously at the platinum star pasted to her pubic bone.

"Hi, Jack," she says.

(To him and him alone. What's he got that I haven't got? What is it about Jake that people would always rather talk to him instead of me? Why is he the chosen one, not just here in America, because it could be that people are *unsure* about me, that I give the impression of being slightly disreputable, not quite nigger, not quite white, a Palestinian among Jews, but back home, too? Nobody sees me.)

"She's not bad, huh?" says Jake.

"Nope."

"Friendly, too."

"Friendly?"

"I mean, she's sitting there scratching her fan-tan and she still calls me Jake!"

Michel feels like throwing up. He looks at the mural on the wall, a prairie landscape with buffaloes and a lasso-throwing cowboy. Buzzards. A setting sun.

Leah prances to the other side of the stage and asks some drunk sitting there what his name is. "Bob." She says she thinks Bob looks like President Carter. Applause and laughter. Bob pulls off his shirt, exposing a fishy-white, muscleless torso, waves his shirt like a flag, and wails the first few lines of "The Star-Spangled Banner," right in the middle of a saxophone solo.

Then Leah comes back. Kneeling down at the edge of the stage, where the carpet is nailed and gnarled, she parts her knees and winks at Jake, who, blushing crimson, winks at Michel.

"What do you think?" he whispers.

"She's crazy about you."

"I think so, too."

Leah's tits are paler than the rest of her amber-colored body; she swings them to and fro.

"She looks a little like that Mama Rachel, the broad with all those leather boys in Los Angeles, remember? Don't you think? Same mouth. They could be sisters."

"This one has duller eyes," says Michel.

Leah spreads her thighs and falls back, as all these broads do, with a practiced flourish (and what if I, just once in my life, what if I were to slip a white-hot sheet of metal on that very spot where she's about to fall with the full weight of her credulous, sweaty body, an incandescent metal slab invisible to any other eye but mine, so that for one, brief moment she'd look, stunned, panic-stricken, at *me*, her grinning god, and *see* me just before her layers of fat are seared, scorched, roasted . . .) Michel dispels the thought, and his hard-on melts when he looks at Leah the way he thinks that Jake and all the rest of these lechers see her, a blond slut thrusting out her belly and groping around in her crotch.

"Cock-a-doodle-doo!" says Jake to Leah.

"Huh?"

"Would you shut up," hisses Michel.

"You wanna little pussy?" she asks.

"Yes," says Jake. "Yes, yes, yes."

"What's your name?" she asks, and lo and behold, there they are, those tiny pink lips, just like in the good old days, remember, Michel?, in the army, in that pub next to the barracks, when we used to roll five-franc coins into that gaping wet nest?

"Jake."

"Jack?"

How quiet they are, this captive audience, they've guessed that something is about to happen, that any minute now something will come gushing out of those quivering folds, a white rabbit, a carp, a model train.

"Come and get it, Jack," she purrs.

"Don't you dare," growls Michel. But the big oaf is already on his feet. He reaches for her, she steps aside, giggling, playful, yet with something pained and frightened in the mist-gray eyes. "Don't," Leah laughs.

Drums and sax. Disapproving, threatening howls from his fellow oglers. Jake climbs up on a chair and then topples over when somebody pulls it out from under him. Hanging on to the edge of the stage, he grabs Leah's ankle. She's trapped. "Let me go, asshole!" she screams.

Michel rushes up to Jake just as two bouncers are about to nab the lighthearted, laughing giant. "Come on, you stupid bastard!" shouts Michel. "We're getting out of here!"

"You're right," says Jake. He shakes off one of the bouncers, wrenches an angry mulatto from his shoulder, and is just about to stroll nonchalantly to the exit when the albino emcee leaps, shrieking, onto his back, and flings his legs around Jake's loins. Jake shudders with disgust. Michael grabs the smooth, prissy collar of the albino's shirt and rips it. "What the—?" cries the albino, arranging his long white tangled hair. "My shirt! My two-hundred-dollar shirt!" Michel knees him in his tight, bulging groin. The

116

audience screams and cheers as the albino huddles at the foot of the stage, tears springing from his eyes.

In the ensuing squabble, during which the two bouncers land, cursing, in the laps of uproariously laughing spectators, Jake's pants pocket rips, and silver dollars and plastic chips roll all over the dusty floor. Jake and Michel kneel, search, gather, push, beat, and kick away greedy hands, are then seized by three burly men in uniform and dragged, with the help of seven or eight other guests, to the exit, as the orchestra strikes up a thunderous mambo.

The air-conditioned police van is parked at the curb. Jake and Michel have to sit on the floor. Through the barred window they can see two greasers trying to lure passersby into the Valley of Dolls. "Right this way, twelve, yes, *twelve*, count 'em, totally nude and *unappareled* goddesses of lust, the show never stops, two drinks for twenty bucks, and I don't mean apple juice, come on in and see 'em the way God made 'em, *au naturel*, count 'em, twelve, that's right, a dozen dazzling deities . . ."

The interrogation takes half an hour. Who are they, why, how, and when did they end up here? Michel answers meekly, Jake nods.

"You know darn well you're supposed to keep your hands off those ladies," says the bronzed, white-haired cop who looks like he's stepped right out of a Western. "The owner of the club is gonna be in big trouble because of this, he could lose his license."

"Keep your mouth shut," Michel whispers to Jake, but it's too late.

"She asked for it!" says the dimwit vehemently, almost furiously, "She said, 'Come and get it, Jack!'"

"Who?"

"Leah, the banjo champ."

"Did she say it, or sing it?"

"She said it. To me."

"Was the band playing at that particular moment?"

"No," says Michel. "Yes," says Jake. In unison.

The other cop has a steady, porcelain gaze that makes Michel nervous, and silky black leather gloves. "You, son," he says, "I don't like you. I've had my eye on you for some time now, since last year, in fact."

Why doesn't Michel protest? He returns the glassy stare, waits. Cars honk. The lights from the club flash on and off.

"You got an olive complexion," drawls the cop.

"So what?" It comes out sounding less confident than Michel means it to.

"One of 'em's heavyset and the other's got an olive complexion," says the cop. "Isn't that right, Steve?"

The white-haired cop doesn't answer.

"The olive-skinned guy's the most dangerous. That's what the description says. You dangerous, my boy?"

Michel shrugs. Doesn't dare look at his watch.

"How 'bout you, Fatso?"

"Dangerous? Me? Who would I want to hurt?"

"You know damn well who. Doesn't he, Steve?"

"Poor helpless girls between Pasadena and Aram, that's who," says Steve.

"Where's your car?"

"We don't have a car," says Michel. That clinches it, he thinks.

"Is that right." Bad move. Steve suddenly looks more alert, more suspicious. The other cop looks like he's about to smile. He leans forward.

"Where d'you guys live?"

"In Ghent," says Michel, who feels his calves starting to cramp.

118

"No, stupid, here, in Vegas!"

"At the Picasso Motel."

"The biggest motel on earth!" says Jake.

"Criminal assault," says Steve.

"They're frogs," says the other cop. "One of the suspects had a foreign accent."

"Frogs?" asks Jake. "Us?"

"Frenchmen," mutters Michel.

"Where were you both last Saturday? Did you happen to stroll down here from the Picasso Motel?" asks Steve, lighting a thin cigar. "Around two in the morning? With a little detour through Paradise?"

"The Paradise Stranglers," says his partner thoughtfully. He places his walkie-talkie in his lap, switches it on, rattles off a number. But nothing, nobody answers.

Fifteen minutes later Jake and Michel climb out of the van into the sultry night air. Steve tells them, in a fatherly tone of voice, "If either of you ever get in my way again, I'll put your balls through the wringer."

"He will, too, I swear it," says the other cop. "Watch out, frogs."

15

MICHEL SLIPS THE CHAIN OFF THE DOOR. "See you later," he says to Jake.

"How late? In an hour?"

"An hour and a half."

"Where?"

"At the roulette table on the left." Michel doesn't even have to say which hotel, Jake always goes to Circus Circus.

Jake gets back to work on the letter he's writing. Just now, when he went out for a minute to go to the bathroom, Michel read the first few lines. "Dear Dina, it's Me again, the Weather here is very warm, I'm unhappy, did You get my Last Letter, when I wrote to You about Desire . . ."

Michel walks along in the stifling heat until he can go no farther; his feet glow in the new high-tops. In a lonely corner of the dark bar at the Pioneer he drops down on a sofa and closes his eyes. He orders coffee, eats a crisp, light cookie. Once, in a far-off provincial town, where they still had shops that sold fresh-baked, fragrant bread and cakes, Frans the Dutchman announced amid scornful sniggers from the Unicorn regulars that he made his wife do her own baking, even though her cookies were tougher

120

and more tasteless than the ones from the bakery, because his kids had a *right* to the smell of freshly baked cookies. "Home is where the hearth is"—that was his motto.

In snatches of hot, restless sleep, Michel dreams up a whole series of winning plays in blackjack. The eight of hearts keeps turning up at the wrong moment, or not at all.

A keno girl with an improbably tall, curly wig taps him on the arm and tells him that sleeping in the bar is prohibited.

"I'm not sleeping," says Michel, and wakes up.

"Then it's okay," she said. "I just wanted to let you know."

He marks five keno tickets, pays her, watches as she goes swaying into the darkness, and as he sits there studying the numbers, distracted, impatient, who should appear, less than five feet away, but the dead Rickabone! It's been a while, he hasn't changed, still wearing the same creased, charcoal suit, still groaning when he sits down, stiffly, on the fake leather sofa across from Michel. Only . . . there's something wrong with his face, the nose and cheeks look slightly melted. And his combed-back hair, glistening with brilliantine, looks thinner, you can see the faint white lines where his scalp shows through.

Michel often used to slick back his hair with the same brand of brilliantine, but it never stayed down for long.

"Our souls are parted, my boy," says Rickabone. "It's sad, but true."

"Cut it out," says Michel softly, gently, because he doesn't want to chase Rickabone away. The dead man shifts about on the sofa, raises his backside, pulls down his pants, pops in a suppository, sighs, and settles back down again, with a growl of contentment. Then he says, in a worried voice, which Michel can't remember ever having heard when he was alive:

"What's the trouble, my boy?"

"I'm so tired."

"You've walked a long way. In those new shoes."

"Yes, Father."

Rickabone looks away, sees nothing. "You've already got two fathers, must I be saddled with that as well? I have no talent for fatherhood, not even in thought."

"I'm not asking anything of you."

"Everything."

"Yes."

Rickabone licks his lips. The air, icy cold, is dry. Outside, the pavement sizzles with heat.

"I walked all the way here," says Michel. (All the way to you.) "And in every store I saw the same junk, ashtrays, copper, silver-plated, nickel-plated, ebony, plastic knickknacks, model cars, sheriff's badges, tape recorders, silk scarves, sheepskins, Indian pots, sheepskin coats, Tyrolean clocks, Indian blankets, posters, mace-guns."

"All these things shall end up in a heap on Judgment Day," says Rickabone. "One big, beautiful heap."

"Jake's getting on my nerves," says Michel.

"You're the one who dragged him along."

"He's got no manners."

"Where could he possibly have learned them?" says Rickabone, just as he would in the Unicorn, stroking the air like the back of a cat.

"When he has to go to the john he starts unbuttoning his fly before he's even left the room."

"Does he?" says Rickabone, lifting the fine lines of his brilliantined eyebrows.

"And he snores."

"That's common knowledge. It's his septum. Needs to be straightened."

"Sometimes he spends three quarters of an hour on the toilet, moaning and groaning. The other day he shouted, 'Get me a chisel!'"

"His father had the same problem. Runs in the family. Speaking of which, how is your mother?"

"Leave my mother out of this," snarls Michel, but there she is, sitting in her grimy little kitchen, you can see the cream-colored water pipes just behind her babbling head, she's knitting a sweater, the pattern she has clipped out of *Marie Claire* is lying in her lap, she hears Rickabone's voice and raises her chins, her piercing eyes search for Michel, who curses and calls for the keno girl. She doesn't come.

Rickabone lets out the gurgling, diabolical laugh that all the Unicorn knows and that usually signals a malicious prank.

"Did you lose tonight?"

"Yes." And Michel confesses. Humbly, guiltily, he lists the plays that should've won, he tells him how and where and when he made the blunders he made, how overconfident he has been, responding too recklessly to the expression on a dealer's face, how he hated that blackjack dealer as if he were a real person.

"Novice," says Rickabone, the man who gambled away his whole, sordid life.

Michel wants to seize his hand and kiss it, but he never did that when Rickabone was alive. Why start now?

Rickabone swallows three pink pills . . . he's perspiring. "I never gave a thought to victory," he says, "nor to defeat, for that matter, but I fought like the devil, to the very end."

"Yes, Father," says Michel, bowing his head. He is overcome

with a vague sense of melancholy, because he no longer believes so strongly in Rickabone's presence.

"Do what you must do," says Rickabone, far away.

"I shall." Michel's bowed neck waits for a caress, a coup de grace.

"Are you that tired?" asks the keno girl.

"No."

"You won," she says, and pays him thirty dollars. He hands her five. She thanks him with a frozen smile.

"Dishonor," says Rickabone as he walks Michel out the door, "Avoid dishonor, at all costs. That's much more important than winning or losing."

Michel grins. As if Rickabone, who, dead or alive, has never stopped peddling the same old samurai laws, weren't the champion of dishonor!

"You're thinking of that unfortunate affair with Markie and dear little Didi," says Rickabone accusingly. "That was a joke! An experiment, if you like. But surely even *you* can see the humor in it."

"And what about your honor?"

"Honor to whom honor is due," says Rickabone.

Michel turns to him and, with a wave of his arm, scatters him to the winds. Then, chuckling, he heads back to the motel.

Verbist the Schoolmaster once called Rickabone a well, a well that could never be filled. (No matter how much I try to remember, no matter how much I imitate, even if I turn into Rickabone himself, I'll always be Michel, a sump, a sewer, at the very most a disagreeable odor in the nostrils of the Unicorn.)

Near the entrance to the motel, Jake is sitting in the whirlpool bath that is usually filled with elderly arthritics. Next to him, a man with sparse reddish curls is floating on his back in the steaming, swirling water.

"Over here!" Jake calls out.

Michel sinks down on a metal chair, exhausted.

Jake is bobbing up and down like a gigantic inflatable rubber doll filled to bursting. The other man raises his head. His chest is covered with curly white hair. He stands up, but doesn't look much taller; he has the legs of a little boy.

"This is Brother Amos," says Jake.

"Hi there!" says a gravelly voice. "Come on in! It's just the thing for a couple of kids like you. Great for the joints."

Michel has seen this Amos before. Just the other day, at Circus Circus, he was standing next to the boxing ring, in which a kangaroo in a bra and lace panties was boxing with three young girls. The boxers were all wearing flat red gloves that looked like seal's flippers. This Amos here was in livery. Jake was standing by his side, Michel remembers, suddenly angry.

"Brother Amos owns a ranch around here," says Jake.

Amos falls face down in the water, snorts, and pops back up to the surface.

"Just sheep," he pants. "No cattle."

"He says we can come hear him preach sometime."

"Well, well. The gentleman preaches," says Rickabone.

"What do you preach about?" asks Michel.

"About praising the Lord! We meet each week in the New Church of The Founders. We're planning to have an outdoor café and squash court built, right on the premises. Of course, that means we'll have to organize a lot more benefit concerts. With God's Trombone. Brother Jethro, that is."

Look at Jake gazing at his new friend! It's sickening. Michel turns away. Rickabone is gone. What would he say? "Michel, my child, above all, you must never be dependent on those you hold dear!" Something like that. Straight out of the samurai handbook.

"Have you run up many debts, my friend?" asks Amos.

"No," Michel replies curtly.

"What's your name, my friend?"

"Michel," says Jake.

"The way they treat people here who, in their weakness, have run up debts . . . I tell you, it's a thorn in the eye of the Lord! They'll sell off all your worldly possessions in half an hour. Right down to your shoes. Believe me, Michel, in this town they turn honest people into junkies. In half an hour! Boozehounds and murderers. Never again will this city rise from its decrepitude. The eyes of the Lord God are upon this sinful kingdom." Amos bursts into song. "He shall destroy this kingdom from the face of the earth, raze it to the ground!"

"That's how he preaches," says Jake, smiling tenderly.

"But my friend Jake here," says Amos, laying a hairy arm around Jake's neck, "he is chosen, he shall be saved by the Lord. Isn't that true, Jake?"

"Oh, yes," says Jake.

Michel walks away. Two prophets: Rickabone, the ghost of destruction, and this Amos, singer and dwarf—it's too much for a man to bear. At the curve in the asphalt road that leads to their room he looks back and sees Amos and Jake splashing water at each other, like a couple of six-year-olds.

16

TWO DAYS LATER IT'S SUNDAY. Michel suggests they fly over the Grand Canyon, one of the World's Greatest Most Wonderful Great Natural Wonders, in an eight-seater plane, thirty-eight bucks, drinks included.

For the first time on this trip, Jake refuses.

"You what?" Michel is dumbfounded.

"We can always just tell 'em we've seen it," says Jake.

"Sure, Jake. When it comes to lying, you're the champ," says Michel.

Jake thinks this over. "I don't lie," he decides.

"Hiding the truth is lying, too."

"I'm not hiding anything. What about?"

"You know a lot more than you're letting on. You've got something up your sleeve, buddy, don't try to fool me. You're not as stupid as you pretend to be."

"What about?"

"We'll discuss it some other time."

"No. Now."

"No. Some other time."

127

"What's it about?"

"About Markie."

Jake's innocent, blank, pleading expression, the hesitant, high little voice, "Markie? What about him?" make Michel uncomfortable. Could it be that Jake really knows nothing (even though he, Michel, has always assumed that he did)?

"Maybe you're right," says Michel. "Maybe it's better to leave some things left unsaid. For our own good," he adds, and disappears into the shower.

Then it turns out that the reason Jake doesn't want to come along to the Grand Canyon is that he has promised to go hear Amos's sermon. They drive over in a cab. Because the roles have been reversed: Michel is now following Jake. He finds it amusing, and strangely satisfying, to let Jake take the lead.

The Church of The Founders is an old barn, patched up and painted lavender, in which a dozen middle-aged men in seersucker suits and twice as many women in gaily flowered dresses greet each other with overly exuberant cries. Jake and Michel stand around looking lost. Two of the ladies smile at them benignly and then go back to swapping recipes.

A glum-looking man in horn-rimmed glasses walks up to a raised platform with a microphone on it and says how truly delighted he is to see so many brothers and sisters gathered here today, but even more so because on this day, two of their foreign brethren have found their way to the Holy Word. Eyeglasses in hand, he gestures vaguely toward Michel. All heads turn and nod amiably at the foreigners; Jake flushes crimson. The speaker says that he will now give the floor to the inimitable Brother Amos, who will inspire them, as only he can, with his pearls of popular wisdom. "And here he is!" Applause.

"Yeah, yeah!" shouts a pimply-faced girl next to Michel. Her fiancé grabs her excitedly in the loins. Amos emerges from a side entrance and walks resolutely, long arms swinging, to the dais. He taps several times on the microphone and then launches into a fiery tirade, his voice swooping and soaring, like an auctioneer at the fish market on the Ostend quay. Jake nods eagerly at the dwarf, as if to encourage him.

"The time is ripe. Oh, Lord, verily, the time is ripe. The habitations of the shepherds shall mourn! The top of Carmel shall wither! The Women of Vegas dress themselves nowadays in men's clothes, with shirts and ties and corduroy pants. I will send a fire on the wall of Gaza which shall devour the palaces thereof! The Women of Vegas have scorned the word of the Lord, forsaking their husbands and embracing one another, so that they are no longer even capable of doing their housework. They can't even make a decent pancake! And the Lord saith, None of them shall escapeth, though they hide themselves in the top of Carmel, I will search and take them out thence. The Men of Vegas—I have beheld them with mine own eyes, for in order to fill my children's bellies I am required to work in their den of iniquity—the Men of Vegas rub their faces with creams and oils to look more youthful and thus please each other. Though they be hid from my sight in the bottom of the sea, thence will I command the Serpent, and he shall *bite* them!"

Amos snaps at the air; his pearly white teeth rattle.

"My brethren, our city is being debauched by lies from the Red East, scarlet idols rule, surrounded by parlor pinks! At this very moment there are three Russian travel agencies in Vegas, and our sentinels lie sleeping, but I will set mine eyes upon them, for evil, and not for good! The name of the Lord has been erased, *erased*, from the schoolbooks of the children of Vegas. Just the other day I saw two innocent, seven-year-old girls making water balloons out of condoms! Oh yes, yes verily, but woe betide you, saith the Lord, The sinners of this people shall die by My sword!"

White flecks appear on his lips. He gives Michel a hateful, devastating glare. He pants, hiccups, and lapses into an almost unintelligible muttering, something about the fallen tabernacle of David, about closing its breaches and raising up its ruins, when the door of the barn crashes open and in walks a tall man in a gray shantung suit, his pants legs tucked into a pair of white boots. A slender young man in a jean suit is leading him forward by the elbow. The tall man holds his upper body as stiff as a board, but his head wobbles dangerously on his neck.

Amos stops in the middle of his narrative, just as it's about to dissolve once again into a flood of imprecations. The speaker jumps to his feet and flings out his arms. The men and women of the congregation nudge each other, whispering excitedly.

"Yes, brothers and sisters," Amos cries, "he's here, in our midst, a Great American Citizen, Brother Jerry Lee Lewis!"

"And *Charles*. Whatever you do, don't forget Charles. Right, Charlie-my-boy?" shouts the tall man. His companion waves to all present and pushes Jerry Lee Lewis toward the dais.

"That's not Jerry Lewis," says Jake. "I saw him on TV, just the other day."

"Jerry *Lee* Lewis."

"Is that somebody else? Are there two of 'em?"

"This one's a singer."

"Why didn't you say so?"

Jerry Lee Lewis is trying to get a cigarette into his mouth. He pokes the filter end against his cheek several times, then flings the cigarette on the wooden floor and scratches his faded curly hair (once a shiny, greased pompadour that adorned millions of album covers). He's unshaven, his bloodshot eyes dart back and forth.

"I promised!" he shouts. "As Charles is my witness, I promised I'd play for you today, here in this godforsaken hole."

"He's left his guitar somewhere," the young man says to the flock.

"Guitar, my ass. I don't play guitar, Dumbo!"

He sits down on the dais, his legs wide apart. "When I make a promise, I stick to it. Even if it costs me a hundred thousand bucks."

"And that's why we love you, Jerry Lee," says the speaker. "We feel blessed that you're doing us the honor—"

"Praise the Lord!" Amos yells hoarsely. "Amen!" cries the congregation.

"I met Charles at the Desert Inn," says Jerry Lee, "and he's been with me ever since." Charles is standing behind him with his arms folded, like a bodyguard for a big-time gangster in a movie. "And now I'm gonna sing for you. Whaauw!" His head wobbles, drops onto his shoulder, he looks like he's about to puke. He throws his head back and yells, "Whaauw!"

"Wauw!" shouts the bitch with the pimples next to Michel. "Jerry!"

"Yeah, sister?"

"Jerry, can I cop your cherry?" All those present smile shyly. There's an expectant silence, which is broken by a slap the girl gets from her fiancé. The young man rubs his wrist.

"I gave away my cherry long ago, sis," says Jerry Lee, with a sly grin.

"Did he bring sherry?" asks Jake.

"*Cherry*, his virginity," says Michel impatiently. Jake is shocked, though he's not quite sure he understands it.

"Gave it away when I was fourteen. To Mary Lou Weintraub, may God roast her alive."

Amos squats down next to Jerry Lee, as if he's about to tie his shoelaces, and whispers in his ear.

"Folks!" cries Jerry Lee. "Amos is right. Time is running out! At this very moment hordes of fans are waiting for me over at the Flamingo, they're fretting and fuming, they're lining up for the Show of the Century, for poor ol' Jerry Lee!"

He strokes the thin curls of the crouching prophet.

"Yes, this old dogface, this douchebag with apeshit for a brain, is right. Time's running out. So here's a song. Dedicated to my Mama. 'That Old Country Church.' He stomps furiously on the wooden floor with his white high-heeled boot. Unaccompanied, the song sounds too loud, and completely off-key, but the congregation hums along, swaying and hopping in place even when Jerry Lee, without any warning, switches over to an old rock 'n' roll number, while the expression on his face remains unperturbed, almost contemptuous.

"That's all, folks," he says. He tries to get up, leaning on Amos's shoulder for support, but flops back down again. Charles takes out a hip flask, drinks, and belches.

"I am a sinner," says Jerry Lee all of a sudden. "Always have been. Amos here, this piece of shit, wants me to confess it in public. Fine with me. Yes, you motherfuckers, ol' Jerry Lee is a sinner. In many a wanton bed has he laid his head and balls to rest. He has gone to great expense to have snow geese mate in his very own garden and then blown them to smithereens with his very own Winchester. Yes, a slave to his passions, that's what he's always been. And still is!" He struggles to his feet, his broad hips shake, his belly jerks up and down. "I'm the Meat-man!" he sings. (I don't like vegetables. Meat, I want meat. Tough old beef or the flesh of young calves, I don't care which. I'm the meat-man.)

"Shake, shake!" cries the pimple-faced girl.

"Yeah, sis, shake, shake!" Jerry Lee chimes in. "God be praised," he says as he sits back down and wipes his brow on the shantung sleeve. He jiggles his right leg a few more times, as if he's trampling the pedals of an invisible piano. Charles yawns.

"I am a murderer," says Jerry Lee quietly. "And I wish to testify to this, here, in this house of God. For I, with my senseless defamations, have driven a man to his death, and that man was the greatest, most patriotic singer in this whole great country, none other than Mister Elvis Presley."

"May he rest in peace!" bellows Amos. "Amen!" shouts the audience at the top of their lungs.

Jerry Lee raises his hand, his platinum bracelet slips down over his sleeve. "I have been jealous, I was possessed by a devil and he made me go to the house of Elvis, and there, in the dead of night, I hurled deprecations at the front wall of that house, behind which Elvis was trying to enjoy his well-deserved sleep. Yes, folks, I did wake him up. Yes, he was obliged to call the police. Yes, I did throw cans of Heineken through his bedroom window. Yes, I did attempt to set fire to his Rolls-Royce. And since that time I have never been the Jerry Lee Lewis I once was. His death was the cruelest punishment that could ever be inflicted upon me. God bless the soul of this great American. Let us pray. You too, Charles."

Everyone bows his head. Jake bows very low. Jerry Lee Lewis's wild, troubled gaze settles on Michel (who once, long ago, let "Big-Legged Woman" and "Night Train to Memphis" thunder through his brain while screwing Verbist the Schoolmaster's wife with his headphones on). You're not praying, Jerry Lee, thinks Michel. Neither are you, thinks Jerry Lee.

Smiling guiltily, Jerry Lee is led away, pale and subdued. "Fuck you all, darlings," he says at the door, as the audience applauds wildly.

"It is the Lord who destroys the fortress, who saps the strength!" Amos starts in again, and the afternoon turns to dusk, filled with profanations. Michel leaves Jake behind in the barn.

17

"**DEAREST DINA,** dearest Didi, the Weather in London is warm but humid too, if it keeps up like this all my clothes will be wet before I even get to America. London is a lot bigger than you'd think because they don't have a Center of Town like we do, but that's enough about London, I want to write about Us, dearest Dina, and about our Dearest darling who I want You to give lots of Kisses from me. You can't kiss her *enough*, Can You, some people, for instance doctors and teachers at Her old school say you have to have Discipline to give the children A Character of Steel for later on when she has to live in Society when We're not around anymore but don't forget that for as long as we still have Each Other We *Can't* say often enough how much We love Each Other. I know I Myself don't always do that either and sometimes I say or do Things I Don't mean, but You know, don't you Dina, that it's not just My Fault."

(Dina has already read the letter from England, twice, but now that she's reading it aloud to Didi, who's sitting and drawing a farmhouse with a locomotive-shaped cloud above it, and hears her own petulant, reluctant voice, it's as if she is reading a different letter, as if the sound is transforming Jake's scrawl into something entirely new, as if someone is telling her something in her own querulous voice that she doesn't yet know, and that someone is a stranger, a cross between Jake and herself, a weak, plaintive face without eyes or mouth.

"No. Not now," she says to the curate when he tries to interrupt her. "I want to read this first." Then, more quietly, "Please.")

"It's not too bad in my Room. My Traveling Companion is sleeping, but not me. I can't, because being away from you and thinking about you both I get really nervus like after I've drunk too much of that coffee you always buy, with the black cat on the package. My Thoughts are as Follows: I'll try to be fair and Honest because I am a true Enemy of Dishonesty. Your Curate knows that too, ask him next time you see him."

(The curate's pipe wobbles up and down. The smell of tobacco is sickeningly sweet. Why don't I just yell at him to get out of my house! thinks Dina.)

"I've been thinking about Desire, Dina. Because we don't have Much More than that, we poor, weak Humens. But it's the Only Thing we do have, that's really Ours, Nothing to Do with our Situation or Politics and all the Big Shoots we see on TV. You see, dearest Dina, dearest Didi! Here I am doing what you always tell me I do, Filosofizing all by my Lonely Self.

"As long as it's True and real, We can't be harmed. All the rest are Sick down to their bones. I'm often Sick too like Them but that comes, Dina dear, from Warmth and from Desire. I have only One Place and that's You, You and My Didi. All the rest is the Enemy. Even my Traveling Companion, who is sleeping like a Guardian Angel. Should I ever have left You? No. Just when My Darling Girl needed me so badly? No."

(Dina notices that Didi, for some time now, has been rubbing her purple crayon back and forth over the roof of the farmhouse, that she's drooling, that she has to pee.)

"Now I'm going to tell You more about My Thoughts, because when I'm Home I never get the chance. The minute I start to say something, a Voice Deep Down Inside Me says, Shut your mouth, Stoopid, first learn how to think serious, and then you can talk. We, Dina, You and I, We never seem to have Time, isn't that True, Dina? If my Bic doesn't dry up I'll keep on writing. I'm not trying to be Deceitful! Deceit is okay for My Traveling Companion, who's always acting like he's a Captain in a War, moving around his Soldiers, His Weapons, His Pieces, like he's playing Chess, or Checkers, or Stratego.

"I don't have to hide from the Two of You. From Him I do. If I say the least little Serious Word he starts laughing at Me. When I try to explane something he gets Nervus.

"It's only lately that I've been hiding from You, Dina, it *wasn't* like that in the beginning when we got married. Remember, when I used to get undressed, how I said to You: look at me, this is it, me in my Nakedness, this is all I have, and it's all Yours, we've had so many laughs and isn't it a crying shame that we've forgotten it over the Years and with all the troubles with our Darling Girl. Is she eating enough? Make sure You buy entrecôtes at Buyltinck's, it's the freshest meat by far and not far from Our house."

("The entrecôte at Vanderhagen's isn't bad either," says the curate. "But the problem with entrecôte is that you always get such a large piece, and for someone who lives alone, like me, it's simply too much . . .")

All this time Didi has been rubbing her middle finger over the purple smudge on her drawing. Dina finishes her cold coffee and starts off on the next sheet of graph paper that has been ripped out of a spiral notebook. Dina is certain it was Michel's, that lowlife.)

"You should also tell her that even though now for the time being She is Different than other peeple because She's not Well, that She's still better than a Lot of Other Peeple that She can see for herself on TV who are suffering from hunger and thirst or Earthquacks or Fashist Generals, and that her Weakness is just a different kind of Strength than Ours, and also that, being a Woman, she shouldn't take our men's affairs too seriously. Also one more thing, you should get her to paint everynight with her Watercolors, because that's good for her, that's a well-known fact."

("What's a well-known fact?" asks Didi.

"What your father says," says Dina.

"What does he say?"

The curate points to her drawing. "Papa means that working with color is good for your mental development. Incidentally, Didi, the application of rays of colored light is also highly recommendable." He pokes an elegantly dancing forefinger into her back. "Look, here's a chakra, just next to your spleen, which attracts orange, and this one, above your kidneys, attracts *yellow*."

Didi rolls a green crayon between her fingers.

"Green," says the curate, "symbolizes nature, equilibrium, and peace. Green suppresses emotional disorders. Green is good for high blood pressure, headache, flu. Indigo, on the other hand—"

"Please," says Dina.

Didi rummages through her wooden box and then, licking her lips, covers the farmhouse with grass-green stripes. Dina notices that her breasts are squashed flat again, under her sweater. Didi binds them with rubber weather stripping. Dina continues reading the letter, slightly louder this time, and more emphatically.)

Desire

"This Desire, it's hard because it's under Your Skin and you only know it's there when it brings you misery, especially to Yourself."

("Yes," says Didi, almost inaudibly. A gasp. Dina immediately goes on reading, faster this time.)

"It's stupid as an Ox, Desire, because it's not only Your Body that reacts. I've been looking at the City of London differently than usual because Desire keeps getting in the way of my eyes, and No becomes Yes and Yes becomes No, it's like Dying, Dina. You probably think I'm whining, don't you? But what else can I do but tell you all this, because if I don't say it, then it Isn't There. Because the real reason I left was so I would be able to say it, you have to go Away otherwise it doesn't work trying to say it, because there's no way I can say it right to Your Face, that's why the distance from London to You At Home in Our Street is the measure of this Desire, that's why I think about Desire more when it isn't there, can you understand? I'll stop now."

("No," says Didi. "There are more pages."

"Three more," says Dina.

"This is extremely interesting," says the curate. "I'm almost tempted to define the anonymity of his desire in transcendental terms. Because one could, theoretically, interpret his desire as a sign of grace."

"Please," says Dina. That's the third time, she thinks. Third time pays all.)

"The only thing I know is that I long to see Desire, long to keep longing for Desire . . ."

(She stops. There's no more coffee in the pot.

"Did he say 'longing' or 'prolonging'?" asks the curate, puffing on his pipe. "He probably means 'prolonging.'"

"I don't know," says Dina wearily. "He's lost his mind."

Didi roars with laughter. It's like an explosion. Her crayons roll off the table.

"Sorry," says Dina. "I didn't mean it like that." Didi stops laughing as violently as she has begun. She sits there panting, her smudged fingers pressed to her lips.

The curate is stunned. He picks up the crayons and, much to Dina's relief, he stands, brushes the ashes off his lap, and says, "Sorry, but I have to be off to vespers. I'll see myself out." He disappears, taking the sickly smell of tobacco with him.

After supper and "Kojak," Dina continues reading. This time there is an even greater gap between the letters she sees and the thin, petulant sounds coming out of her mouth. Didi, a glass of chocolate milk in her hand, stares fixedly at her bruised knees, waiting for a scab to form so she can pick it off again.)

"What I'm trying to say can't be said, but it's the Not Saying It that's the Desire. Is it Desire for You? For Us? For the whole World, where I'm dying a little more every day? The more I think about the World the more I see it in so many different ways and most of all the unhappiest. Don't you ever get that sometimes, Dina? But now I think I'll put down my Bic. I've got finger cramps."

("There's still two more pages," says Didi.)

"Why does Michel look down on me? Like you do? Because it's fun? Because it makes you laugh? I'm a Persun, a hundred percent, from top to bottom. And you, Dina, you look down on one part, one Particle of me. I'm all alone in my loneliness, and the whole time you're having fun and looking down on me. A lot of the time, anyway. But sometimes Your Desire clashes with my Desire. It used to, anyway. But these days my Desire is mostly just Dead Weight, 250 pounds worth, give or take a few, and I spit on them, on all those Pounds when I Think of how you can't, don't *want* to love me anymore, a lot of the time, anyway. And the same goes for my little Didi . . ."

("Not Didi!" screams Didi. "Please!"

"Quiet! Hush, come now," says Dina. But it's too late, Didi is drumming on the table, kicking the table legs, bellowing, "Not Didi! No, motherfucker, not Didi! No, shit, piss, poop, shove it up my ass, *no!* Not Didi!"

Dina wants to call out for the curate's help, but he isn't there. She tries to restrain the flailing Didi but the girl is as strong as a horse and shoves her mother up against the wall, pins down her wrists, and starts licking her face. Dina doesn't move. Whatever you do, Dina, just keep looking her straight in the eye.

Growling, Didi releases her and starts to dance. It's a boogie-woogie, like she used to do not so very long ago when she would climb out the window at night and not come home till dawn and then dance alone in the kitchen and hum the songs she had heard on the jukebox in those disgusting bars where the young people go. When she was well.

Didi dances more slowly. Then she sits back down at the table and slashes the grass-green farmhouse with streaks of bloody red.)

18

THE BETRAYAL, because as far as we're concerned there's no other word for it, occurred on the night of the Trade Union Dinner. Who was there? Too many to mention. 'Cause if there's a free meal to be had, even if it's only a bowl of mixed pickles, nearly everyone shows up. Who wasn't there? Salome, Doctor Verbraeken and Markie, the Three Graces. And it was just as well.

If you've got a minute I'll explain to you how it all came about, that Trade Union Dinner.

Deaf Derek, who incidentally is no deafer than you or I but is called that because he always has to think so frightfully long and hard and deep before drawing a card, used to live, I think we can safely say without affronting him, in a dump. The top floor looked like something left over from the bombing of Merelbeke, when the Brits were aiming for the station and ended up wiping out the whole town instead. There weren't many of us at the Unicorn that shed a tear the day Churchill choked on his last cigar.

Derek's roof was full of holes, the doors sagged, all the windows were smashed, in short, it was a disgrace. And over the years a whole colony of pigeons had nestled there. But Deaf Derek and his wife, Marguerite, didn't lose any sleep over it. On the contrary! It made them feel as if they were living in the country, but then right in the center of town. Hearing those pigeons coo-cooing every morning, said Marguerite, was certainly a lot more agreeable than listening to Derek snore! Derek fed them, stale bread and corn. Sometimes he'd spend the whole afternoon sitting up there with those pigeons, but only if Marguerite wasn't home, of course, because she can be, if you'll forgive me for saying so, troublesome. Change of life, you know. And jealous by nature. No, jealous isn't quite the right word. Possessive, clingy, overly affectionate—how can I explain? "Derek, where are you, lovey? Derek, my lamb, what're you doing? Derek, Derek, why won't you answer me? You were a lot nicer to me when we were courting!" And so on. You know the type.

Well, the last few months Marguerite's mother had been having trouble with her blood pressure, so one day Marguerite says, "Derek, my precious, wouldn't it be a lovely idea if Mama moved in with us? She could live upstairs, on the top floor, she'd have someone to look after her and a bit of companionship and at eight o'clock in the evening we'd just shut the door to the hallway and we wouldn't hear a thing." "Fine with me," says Derek, who naturally was thinking of the inheritance, because Marguerite's got two brothers and three sisters and they're all tugging at their mother's pursestrings. Okay. So Derek points the bricks, puts in new windows, papers all the walls. But, sir, those pigeons! A pigeon, sir, may be clever enough to fly from Montpellier to Ghent, to coo and screw, but for the rest a pigeon is a bit of a birdbrain. Those damn pigeons, who had been making their nest on the top floor for years and years, kept trying to get back in. They'd sit up on the roof for a while doing their business and then fly right smack into the windowpanes. Every now and then one of 'em would hit the pavement.

Now, just across the street from Deaf Derek's house is the Catholic Trade Union Building, one of those big modern rock-piles that sullies our noble skyline (but never mind, what can you expect with a town council like ours), and that Union Building is full of lazy good-for-nothings who sit around all day staring out those big, modern windows. They've got nothing better to do than chew on their pencils and talk about Sport Weekend on TV. Or stare out the window. "Why look, Mister Chief of Staff, a cloud!"—"Why yes, Mister Octave, perhaps we're in for some rain."—"Now that you mention it, Mister Edgar . . ."

Which meant that all the goings-on with those wretched, rest-less pigeons across the street were, for them, the spectacle of a lifetime. The place was in an uproar! The whole damn Union stood at the window and was outraged at what it saw. It held an emergency meeting and sent over a delegate. Derek had to open his windows, said the delegate, because torturing and tormenting pigeons was simply not allowed. "But, sir," says Derek, "they're not *my* pigeons."—"Sir, you either see to it that those pigeons can get in, or build them a new dovecote! But one way or the other, those birds must be saved."—"Sir," says Derek, "you can kiss my ass."

Discussions, debates. The Society for the Prevention of Cru-elty to Animals, the town council, the police. There were some who threatened to go to the Council of Europe. Signatures were collected, from various syndicates, soccer clubs, cultural societies. There was even talk of holding a picket march outside Deaf Derek's door. That's right, sir, just like they did for that business over in Chile, with all the torturing.

The commissioner of the sixth precinct was embarrassed. "Derek," he says, "this whole thing is turning into a political affair! Do something about it, do it for me, as a friend."

"Okay, Mister Commissioner," says Derek. "I do hereby swear to take those pigeons under my wing." He went upstairs, threw open his windows, and the whole flock of pigeons flew inside.

And that's how we ended up with pigeon *à la diable* on the menu that night at the Unicorn. Two pigeons apiece.

Felix the Cat did the birds; that is to say, he supervised, he gave the orders, in a long white apron and chef's hat (this was no laughing matter), and the others had to chop the pigeons in half, pound them flat, bind up all those little wings under all those little legs. Verbist the Schoolmaster, who usually got buttermilk mush for supper at home, tried to interfere with the preparations but was shooed out of the kitchen, and it was Staf van't Peperstraatje who assisted Felix with breading the birds and rubbing 'em in with Tierenteyn mustard. Melted butter over the top, thirty minutes under a slow grill, and a good douse of "pungent pigeon sauce," as Staf proudly called it: shallots, white wine, ketchup, and plenty of cayenne pepper.

So there we are having our supper. Frans the Dutchman has already finished his two pigeons and is leering at potential leftovers on other people's plates, when all of a sudden the door flies open with a bang that makes everyone look up. Because the Unicorn regulars, even dead drunk, are always real careful opening the door so as not to break the antique stained glass or, even more important, the players' concentration. And who should be standing there, for the first time ever in all her life? Dina, Jake's wife.

Now, I can't look into other people's souls, but seeing as how we at the Unicorn know our neighbors right down to the core, I'd honestly have to say that every one of us Unicorners had clean forgotten about Jake and Michel on those foreign shores. They were never mentioned. We didn't even recognize Dina at first, because on top of everything else she looked like she'd just risen from Purgatory. White as death, her hair in her teeth, huge, blue-rimmed eyes, a scornful sneer on her lips. And looking around to see whom she should devour first.

"Well, look who we have here!"

"A body would pay money to see you!"

"Pull up a chair, Dina darling."

"It's pigeons *à la* Felix the Cat."

"Followed your nose, eh?"

"Here, Dina, have a wing."

But she just stands there, searching among us for someone who isn't there.

Gerald the Prick, our professional ladies' man, sidles up to her, wipes the sauce from his lips with his paper napkin before he speaks, and says, "Dina, my angel, I've been waiting for you all evening. How could you put me through such agony?"

A load of eyewash, of course, but the curious thing is that whenever Gerald the Prick, with his Clark Gable moustache and his old-fashioned, conspiratorial smile, spouts such drivel, the women listen. Sure enough, Dina takes off her raincoat, sits down, drinks a pale ale, eats half a pigeon, we ask her for news of Jake, she tells us she's had only one letter in all that time and that one was sent from London, probably took so long to arrive because the bloody English are on strike again, and we nod, because that's what you get when the unions rule a kingdom.

Actually it was because of that letter, she says, that she got up the nerve to come down here, because when she read her daughter the letter the poor girl got so nervous that it was urgent that

Doctor Verbraeken come straight away, and she thought she might find him here in the Unicorn.

Doctor Verbraeken might drop by later on, we tell her. Should we call Doctor Grootjans in the meantime? He's more of an ear, nose, and throat man, of course, but if it's an emergency . . .

"No," says Dina. "It has to be Doctor Verbraeken, he knows her case." Mister Jules, the dachshund, sinks his teeth into her coat sleeve and won't let go. At that very moment, at another table, Frans the Dutchman breaks into the Flemish national anthem and we can steer the conversation in another direction. Fortunately for us, because we feel awkward, powerless in the face of Didi's fate, Didi, that poor little lamb who lost her way, all because of love. It could happen to any of us, of course, but not as easily. Or as violently. Mercilessly.

Later on, five or six of us, including Dina, go round to the Saint Tropez, where Helène serves us a little something to ease the digestion, since those pigeons really were rather filling. Dina drinks one pale ale after another. Helène comforts her. As we roll the dice we overhear Dina saying she had to tie her daughter to the bedposts, even after putting three sleeping powders in her chocolate milk.

"Hey, hey, Dina," says Helène. "Don't let it get you down. Have another ale, on the house."

"Drinks all around!" cries Frans the Dutchman.

"Not on your life, Dutchy," says Helène. "Just for this poor soul, who's feeling so low because of all your filthy messing about."

"*My* filthy messing about?"

"*All* of yours," says Helène fiercely, "and believe me, I ought to know."

We protest. *Our* filthy messing about? But of course we can't prove our innocence, because that'd blow the lid off the whole damn can of worms and we just couldn't do that to Dina or, *a fortiori*, as Verbist the Schoolmaster would say, to our old pal Jake. Fortunately Helène realizes this too and starts talking about her juicer, the damn thing's broken, she can't make screwdrivers with real orange juice anymore, she has to used canned, like they do in America. But Dina's a woman. She knows something's up. She listens to Helène's waffling, nodding her head now and then, but in the meantime that strange smile has reappeared that she had when she burst into the Unicorn, and she looks us over, one by one. We go on playing, Frans the Dutchman throws three snake eyes, twice, Staf van't Peperstraatje tries, as usual, to erase a few too many chalk marks from the scoreboard, and we're just thinking about heading back to the Unicorn, to our own safe, warm, stinking nest, when Dina starts acting silly and asks Gerald the Prick to dance. During a slow number we see her kissing his neck in the mirror. But we can't just drag him away by the hair and kick him out the door, though we'd like to, because that's when it happens, right before our very eyes: that charlatan Gerald the Prick, coquettish, horny as a toad, thinks that Dina, the clever bitch, is crazy about him like nearly every other female on earth, and we can only stand around and watch, helplessly, as he *betrays* us. We can't hear what he's saying, but we see Dina's grin growing stiffer and colder as she plays piano on his shoulder blade, and something grim, triumphant, that seems to shake her from head to toe. Her blue-rimmed eyes are open wide. The jukebox stops playing.

"Lads, shouldn't we be on our way?" asks Staf van't Peperstraatje, in the overpowering silence.

"Why?" says Dina. "Just when I'm finally enjoying myself."

"To tell you the truth, I *was* thinking of closing early for a change," says Helène. Verbist the Schoolmaster wants to put on a new single, but Dina leans her butt right up against the jukebox and blocks the coin slot. Are those her teeth gnashing? No, it's Helène cracking her knuckles, the mark of a frustrated woman, according to Gerald the Prick.

"You bastards," says Dina.

"You tell 'em," says Helène (who we once saw marching in a demonstration in the marketplace, pro abortion, I believe it was).

Gerald the Prick, who senses our accusatory rage, says, in an unconvincingly soothing tone of voice, "You shouldn't lump us all together, Dina dear. We're not all to blame for what one or two . . ."

Dina's eyes grow wider, she's crying. Helène, that mother hen, strokes her hair and hands her half a glass of pale ale, Dina chokes on it and sits down, coughing and sniveling, in the plush armchair where some of us, from time to time, like to dandle Helène on our knee.

"You knew all along, didn't you?" Dina bursts out at Helène. "Just like the rest of 'em!"

"I know so many things," says Helène resignedly.

"Last round, lads! What'll it be, Dina?" shouts Staf van't Peperstraatje.

"A pale ale," says Dina. Hunched over, distracted, she says, more to us than to Helène, "I've never really wanted to know, who it was, I mean. Not when she was happy. Not afterwards either. 'Cause I was afraid I'd give in to something terrible inside me, heap all the blame on the scum that'd done this to Didi, just to wash away my own guilt. Oh, I was curious, of course. When she was still well, I used to hit her. Oh yes. When she'd be sitting there in the kitchen, stoned out of her mind and laughing after she'd come home from one of those pubs at the crack of dawn.

Laughing like an idiot. Or dancing. I knew she was sleeping with somebody. That she was on the pill. That there may even have been more than one man. I slapped her till her cheeks turned red. Who? Who? Even though I didn't, absolutely did not want to know. Even though I was glad she wouldn't tell, no name, no place, no time. She just stood there laughing like an idiot and her clothes all stinking of pot. Jake never noticed, he's crazy about her but he doesn't even know what kind of dresses she has, or sweaters, what color lipstick she's wearing, just like I don't know anything about him either, it's finally hit me after all these years. I mean, why else would he be writing me such things? Why haven't I ever heard him say anything like that before? Maybe I've just forgotten, maybe he said the exact same things at the beginning, when we first got married, and I just wasn't listening. And now, the very first time he goes away, I have to hear these things from the other side of the world. Sometimes I think I ought to get down on my bended knees and thank that scumbag Michel for taking Jake with him to America. Okay, another pale ale, Helène. Thanks.

"That morning Didi came home at the usual time and I didn't notice anything strange about her except the smoke in her eyes, but that was normal in those days, and it was only when she walked right past me into the kitchen like I was a piece of furniture that I thought, She's going to fall over. 'My head's killing me,' she said and she started groping around like she was trying to find a wall. I gave her an Alka-Seltzer, but she spit it out. So I made her oatmeal because she usually ate three bowls full, Didi did, with brown sugar, she's crazy about oatmeal 'cause my mother always used to give it to her as a child, but she didn't want any, so I'm standing there with the bowl and she moves backward till she's standing with her back against the sideboard and I see she can't speak, her mouth's flapping open and shut. 'What is it, sweetie?' I ask, 'There's nothing to be scared of,' and that was the very last time she looked at me like a child, like a real person, she goes upstairs and three minutes later I hear her lowing like a cow, the whole neighborhood heard it, I went racing up to her room and her teeth were chattering like castanets, I shoved a hankie in her mouth, and then she lay down, stiff as a board, not another peep out of her, and she lay there like that for two whole months. Intravenous feeding, radiation treatments, injections, Doctor Verbraeken, an army of doctors and psychiatrists, but she's never been the same since. It's a *phenomenon*, say the doctors. Like she's some sort of a freak in a circus."

"*Final* last call!" shouts Verbist the Schoolmaster, and he puts on his record. It's "Puppy Love." Very appropriate, but Dina pays no attention. Helène glares at us with undisguised contempt.

19

WHILE MICHEL IS STUDYING the composite picture in the *Las Vegas Sun* (a coarse, ox-eyed oval with eyebrows that meet at the bridge of the nose and symmetrical, rectangular-shaped lips) of one of the Paradise Hill Stranglers, the one with the olive complexion, and feeling a strange affinity with the blank face without pores, pimples, or stubble that, according to the *Sun*, a hundred and eighty policemen are hunting day and night, a face that seems more like a sum of clues, enumerations, and vague details than the face of a man with murderous tendencies, or any other passions for that matter, and while he quickly converts the price of the reward into some four million Belgian francs, Jake is lying, as he so often has in the last few days, on the quaking, rumbling bed that has been tickled into motion by the mysterious mechanism of the Magic Fingers, which, if you can believe the copper plate on the side of the bed, provide fifteen minutes of relaxing bed massage for 25 cents, swiftly transporting the user to a Land of Blissful Tranquility. The last few days Jake seems to prefer depositing his quarters in the Magic Fingers slot than in the slot machines at the casinos. Even though, all in all, he hasn't lost very much so far. Jake never plays according to any law of probability. Come to think of it, he has no strategy whatsoever. He just makes wild guesses—a capricious, sometimes wayward young lad at a country fair. The power of innocence, Michel decides. Something has got to be done about it. Innocence must not prevail.

"What do we do now?"

"Two more minutes," says Jake with his eyes closed. His white body shakes. Lying there with his hands folded on his chest, he looks like a corpse on a marble slab that doctors are trying to bring back to life with a series of rhythmical electroshocks. The bed rumbles, and falls silent. Jake eases himself up and trims his toenails.

"Yes, what do we do now?" he says. The first few days in Vegas a question like that would never have entered their minds. It must be time to leave. The damage is minimal.

"Just one more shot at the big bucks," says Michel. "One last game of Texas hold-'em. I've got to break even, at least."

"Okay, boy," says Jake.

They paddle around in the swimming pool, watch an old movie on TV, in which a doughy-faced blonde looks back on her past every ten minutes to the accompaniment of a heartrending theme song and finally ends up killing herself. The music swells as she plunges from coal-shaped rocks into a raging sea.

They play manille, but their hearts aren't in it.

"We still need this?" asks Jake, holding up a bottle of suntan oil.

"Not me," says Michel.

Jake pours the oil out onto the blue stone threshold of their room and rubs it in with a bath towel. He polishes the stone until the whole thing shines. "There, that's much better," he says.

His bare foot with the tiny toenails glides back and forth over the threshold. "Jake was here, the Flemish Giant, and he left the place cleaner than he found it."

Two more days in Las Vegas, two more days in Los Angeles, thinks Michel. Any longer than that I don't think I could stand. I'll be back, but next time, I'm coming alone.

At last it's dark and they make their way back to the thin, cold, chemical air of Circus Circus. Michel feels a sharp pain above his eyebrows, probably the shock of going from heat to air-conditioning. (No, it's Jake, that 250-pound ball-and-chain around my leg. Why have I gotten myself into this? Serves me right, I can't play this way, I'm not playing tonight.)

As Jake and Michel enter the poker rooms they are amazed to see, sitting at one of the tables, dressed in a dealer's uniform and looking dignified and unapproachable, Jake's friend Amos. Seated, he is just as tall as the other dealers; nothing about the broad torso belies his thin, fragile underpinnings. The table is busy. Amos shuffles and deals efficiently, impersonally, like an old hand.

"Now's our chance," says Jake.

"What do you mean?"

"Look who's dealing!"

"Forget it," says Michel.

"I'm playing."

"Even if he could fix the cards, which he can't, he's still more likely to cheat you than one of his fellow Americans."

"Not Amos," says Jake and sits down.

"Hi, Amos," he says. Amos nods at him as if he's a stranger. "Do you wish to play, sir?" His voice sounds noncommittal, unfamiliar.

154

"You bet!" Jake exclaims.

Without the least sign of recognition Amos proceeds to deal the most devastating cards. Jake loses sixty dollars, a hundred and ten. Smiling incredulously at Amos's right hand with the colorless zircon on the middle finger, Jake gets up. "Thank you, Amos," he says.

"My pleasure, sir," says the dwarf.

And then, because he thinks he sees a fleeting look of relief, like a shadow, flicker across Amos's face, because he wants to teach Jake a lesson, because it is, after all, a singular coincidence and omen that the preacher has emerged this evening as an Accomplice of Sin, because there's something greedy tingling in his midriff, Michel takes a seat at the gaming table, next to a sunburnt, sleepy-looking fellow in shirtsleeves who absentmindedly piles up little stacks of chips, knocks them over, and piles them back up again.

"Don't stand *behind* me," says Michel. Feigning indifference, Jake skirts around the other tables, buys three Bountys at the gift shop and then stands there, chewing, a few feet away from him, in a row of Japanese tourists. He notices how cautiously Michel is playing, letting innumerable chances go by, quick to fold, never flinching, whether he wins or loses.

Michel loses.

Jake is starting to feel hungry again. He tries, with a discreet wave of his hand, to get Michael's attention, but it's no use. Players come and go. Of the first few players Michel and the man in shirtsleeves are the only ones left. The man taps mechanically at his six stacks of chips.

Amos takes out an ivory-white atomizer and sprays a fine cloudlet between his neck and shirt collar. He wipes off his hands on a Kleenex, takes a deep breath, and waits for someone to bring him a new deck of cards. Only now does he seem to recognize Michel. "You're not doing too badly, are you, sir?"

"Not too badly, Amos," says Michel. "I see you've been promoted."

"Oh, this is kind of a sideline for me," says Amos. "I had the night off—the kangaroo got sick. Nothing serious. Stomach bug. But an animal like that is very delicate, you know. And much too valuable for the management to take any chances."

Jake tries to push his way forward and get involved in this friendly chat, but the cards are already being dealt. Michel seems to be bracing himself, peering closely at his cards, a look of grim determination on his face.

(The moment of truth. I can't let myself think about it. Something inside me is humming, something only I can hear. Come on. Come on, you mangy dealer, what've you got for me? Two aces. Bravo. Yes. Way to go. I bet a hundred bucks. Turn 'em up, Amos, come on. Yes. Ace of hearts, jack of clubs, seven of hearts. Thanks a lot, asshole. The winner, that pig-faced plumber with his stacks of chips, is nodding. Of course. Of course he'll call. A hundred bucks. His turn. I raise another hundred. Two aces in my hand, and in front of me another one of those juicy red aces, a steamrolled heart, just the way they're supposed to be. Three aces. Come on. Amos turns up a three of clubs. Three, three aces, someone's singing inside me. I don't want to see the man next to me, not even smell him. What's he doing? Yes, I knew it, that Yankee Doodle cowboy with the corrugated neck is going to call. Okay, boy. A hundred bucks. Come on, Amos, Brother Ballscratcher, something nice for your brother, just draw that last ace, you don't *have* to, I've already got three but you never know, you holier-than-thou asshole. A deuce of hearts. That makes

156

three hearts, three of clubs, jack of spades. How much money have I got left? Don't think. It's gotta flow. Like a rich, velvety gulp of milk. I'm raising. See, Amos, you yokel? Three hundred bucks. My pal here is pretending he has to think about it, the buttermilk in his all-American dickhead orders him to pay up, three hundred bucks, he lays down—yes! bravo!—another three hundred. Don't think. No, don't let a single thought cross your mind. Damned if I'm going to wire Salome for money. No. I call. I'd love to whip out my money with a casual flourish, but my pants are too tight. Here, my last, hot, disgusting, delectable dollars. Three hundred. Come on. Come on. Shoot. Lay it up. Pants down. Show me. NO. Rickabone laughs. He remains invisible, but gasps out his wheezy little snore of a laugh. Oh, my foolish, damnable aces. No!)

Jake sees Michel's lips swell up, a babyish pout, a face like death.

"Sorry, partner," says the man in shirtsleeves, scratching his blue stubble with a chip. (He had a four of hearts and an eight of hearts the whole damn time. Five of one suit. The eight of hearts. The eight of hearts!)

"Do you wish to continue, sir?" asks Amos, unmoved.

"No," says Michel. A headache rolls up from his eyebrows, ripples over his skull, and nestles in the back of his neck. He gets to his feet, mumbling, "See you around, Amos," and holds out his hand.

The dealer with the broad shoulders and thin reddish curls looks at the hand, then past it. "Sorry, sir, we're not allowed to shake hands with the customers."

Jake follows Michel out. "Just don't go telling me it's my fault."

"I didn't say it was," whispers Michel.

"At least you're lucky in love," says Jake. Michel stops so

abruptly that Jake crashes into him. Michel's dark, contorted face stammers out something unintelligible.

"It's not *my* fault," says Jake.

Blindly, the din of a jingling jackpot in his ears, Michel marches out, straight through a pair of velvet curtains, into a long corridor with photographs and posters, a row of glass and aluminum display cases. He slows down and blows his nose, to ease the pressure in his pounding temples.

"How about getting something to eat? I'll pay."

Michel nods. He'll wire Salome. "Pimp, murderer, send check via Lloyds for ten, no five thousand dollars or the Secret Police'll eat your balls for breakfast. Signed: Michel, who knows everything."

The syrupy music filtering through from the casino, against a background of metallic rustling and chinking and buzzing of voices, sounds sharper here, slimier. (If I die, my mother will mourn. Maybe Jan, her husband, will, too, fifteen minutes or so. I haven't lived. I'm not alive now. Not nearly as alive, at least, as that waddling, gleefully innocent creature over there, gazing into a glass case and feeling hungry, which means he's alive, expects something.)

"Hey, look at that!" Jake points to a violin that, according to the card on the wall, is made out of more than twenty thousand matches. Next to it is a drum made out of a human skull, the skull of a Tibetan saint.

"Could you lend me some cash tomorrow?" asks Michel. "I've kind of exceeded my limit."

"Sure," says Jake. With shrill cries, approving growls, astonished expletives, he examines the contents of the display cases. Several times Michel has to help him translate the descriptions. A goat with two heads, a lamb with seven legs, one heart, and two alimentary canals, something that, a hundred years ago, was thought to be a mermaid, the dark, wizened, yawning head of a monkey that has been cleverly and skillfully sewn onto the body of a fish. The Last Supper, just like the real thing, made out of six thousand postage stamps.

"Come here!" cries Jake, the moneylender, and Michel obeys. In the glass case is a wax model of Charles Charlesworth, a stooped old man with owlish spectacles and dusty white hair, supporting himself on a walking stick two feet longer than he is. Born in 1829. Sprouted a moustache at the age of four. His skin wrinkled and shriveled when he was five. At the age of six he began shaking and walking with a stoop, his hair and beard turned white as snow. He fainted one day and died, completely calcified, an old, old man, when he was barely seven.

"Can you beat that," murmurs Jake. Michel hears his stomach growling.

Plennie Wingo, who hiked through Europe backwards, not once but twice, with the help of a rearview mirror. The Iron Maiden. The shrunken heads of the Jivaro Indians, who used to peel the skin off human skulls and boil it down to a third of its original size. Lin Min, the man with the double pupils.

"It's real educational," says Jake. "I can't wait to tell this to Dina and Didi."

"I'm going home," says Michel.

"Good idea." The casino's plate-glass windows are dull gray.

It's morning, but the sky is the color of clay, as if there's a storm brewing. The pockmarked, the lame, the obese war vets with no legs go on playing. Young women who have gambled away all their money yawn and smile at older men, their smiles flashing on and off like the neon lights at the entrance.

Behind the swimming pool pumps, drunken teenagers are lolling around in the plastic grass.

Jake and Michel walk past a khaki-colored Landrover with no wheels. On the windshield, in translucent white letters, are the words BUY ME.

(In Egypt it was at least as hot as it is here, but not as humid, the narrow streets smelled of oil and spices and shit, the muezzin croaked out his jibberish over the rooftops. That kid, told me his name at least three times but I can't remember it now, something Arabic with a *ch* and an *i*, weighed over two hundred pounds, couldn't have been more than fourteen, he was wearing a striped djellaba, he had a frog face with hungry, pleading, disgustingly pulpy wet lips, nothing at all like mine, no way, the panels of his djellaba flapped against his legs. Please, mister, fuck me! he cried. He had sand in his eyelashes. He looked like he'd just been let out of a cage in a cellar where they were fattening him for the kill. One dollar, please! he cried, and later, No dollar, please mister, I love you, fuck me! It was in Egypt, not that long ago. He waited three days until I came out of the hotel, hobbled along beside me, I walked as fast as I could, sweat pouring down my face, after a while he couldn't keep up, his cries followed me through the winding streets, not loud, but intimately, bestially close by, Fuck me, please, buy me!)

That morning they eat turkey with mint sauce in a diner. "Turkey 'n' toothpaste," says Jake. "How do they come up with these things?"

That morning they drink beer and play manille in their motel room. Jake says, "Don't you feel much more at home here than in those casinos? Those stupid casinos. I wouldn't care if we took the next plane back to Belgium."

"I wouldn't care if we'd left ages ago," says Michel.

That morning, when they're about to go to bed and Jake's in

his yellow-checked pajamas but still doing his calculations and entering them in his notebook and Michel has just hung the plastic DO NOT DISTURB sign on the doorknob to ward off the loudly singing maid, that morning, the telephone rings, and after a bit of unintelligible screeching between the operators, it's Dina on the line.

"Jake, is that you?" Her flustered voice is close by, as if she's standing in a phone booth around the corner.

"Yes. Dina. What's the matter? Is something wrong with Didi?"

"She's asleep."

"Ah. That's a relief."

"How are things in America?"

"Fine. But strange."

"I can't stay on long. Only three minutes."

"What's wrong, Dina? Tell me. Please."

"I had to tell you, I couldn't wait. It's keeping me awake at night. I have to— (Her voice is drowned out by boisterous laughter and dance music. She's phoning from a pub.) —And they all say so: it's Markie."

"Markie? Did he have an accident?"

"I wish to God he had!" (She laughs like a young girl. Then there's a stifled coughing sound, right next to the phone.) "Jake, how much longer will you be gone?"

"Four more days."

"Jake, it's Markie that ruined Didi."

"Di-di-did what?"

"Ru-ined her. They told me all about it, those bastards from the Unicorn."

"Who?"

"Staf and Felix and Helène."

"How?" (The background noises fade, the pub has emptied out.)

"How, what?"

"How'd you know I was here? My phone number?"

"Mister Salome told me. The biggest motel on earth, he said. He helped me get the number. But I didn't tell him I knew about Markie, of course."

"Of course."

"Jake, I've got to hang up. You mustn't ever go away again. Do you hear me, Jake? Never again."

"Me neither," says Jake impatiently, confusedly, he has to say something, he says the first thing that comes to mind, then wishes he hadn't.

"Hey. Thanks, Jake."

"Okay," says Jake.

"I'm hanging up now. Hurry back."

"Okay." Squeak.

Jake sits there with the phone in his hand, the black rubber cord stretched out as far as it can go. He taps the receiver against his knee, against his chin.

"It was Markie," he says. He hangs up the phone, shuts his notebook, puts it in the night table drawer next to his *Penthouse* and *Bare Bottoms*, sits down on the edge of the bed, and stares at the floor.

"Markie, he's the one who screwed up Didi."

It's a question, a prayer.

Michel doesn't answer. What he'd really like to do right now is switch on the TV and watch the splotchy, stridently colored commercials, or fifteen minutes of push-ups, exercises for the abdomen and calves, twenty sideways kicks to the larynx of Amos in his dealer's uniform. When he looks at Jake he is amazed to see no sign of rage in the distraught face, just a wide-eyed, woebegone innocence.

"Jake."

"Leave me alone." Jake stuffs a whole Mars bar in his mouth. Michel turns on the TV. A baseball game. He can never make head or tails of this sport. He draws the curtains. The picture doesn't get any clearer.

"Who told Dina?"

"Felix and Staf. Leave me alone."

The truth, tangible, visible, is there with them in the room. As real as the notebook in which Jake records his winnings and losses in childish round figures. Or the fake checkbook that Michel is now thumbing through and that you get every morning for free at the reception desk of the biggest motel on earth.

The checkbook is printed in yellow, cobalt blue, brick-red. That's a fact. That's true. Backgrounds, causes, hidden meanings can do nothing to change that. The letters on the cover look as if they've been painted on with a brush. Motel Guest Book. Model Ghost Book. In the upper right-hand corner sits a gnome with spindly legs and thistledown hair. Written across his chest are the words HA HA! HAVE FUN! ANYTIME!

The book contains a voucher for a free cocktail when you buy two dollars' worth of playing money. A voucher for a clear plastic cup full of chips and nickels worth twelve dollars, for only six bucks. You're bound to win the jackpot with nickels like that! A voucher for a free soft drink of a greenish hue; the glass with the two bent straws twinkles with ice cubes and silver stars. A voucher for free champagne from 8 to 11 P.M. All you can drink at the Silver Fountain. A voucher that's really a raffle ticket, first prize: a trip for two to Palm Springs, adults only. Vouchers for a thirty percent discount on breakfast, including rolls, fruit juice, and a bottomless pot of coffee.

Outside, the sky is leaden. There's a storm brewing. The gigantic neon cowboy hat shows up as clearly as it does at night.

Michel turns off the TV and crawls into bed. Jake just sits there on the edge of his bed, staring at the floor. For a long time the only sound, apart from the thin, syncopated voices of the maids outside the door, is his heavy breathing, the rustling of toffee wrappers, and the occasional fart.

"It's true," says Michel in the gathering darkness. The breathing quickens.

"Of course, if it wasn't Markie it would've been somebody else," says Michel. "Anybody at all. 'Cause in those days Didi used to walk around like a bitch in heat, you know that, Jake. She was asking for it. But it could've been worse. I mean, the guy whose fault it was could've been a much worse kind of guy than Markie, who's not a bad person at heart. You could even say: Hey, they were just a couple of kids! The fact that Didi, when Markie told her it was over between them—and knowing him he probably wasn't too tactful about it, 'cause he was up against the wall— the fact that Didi felt her whole system full of nerves and glands and brains suddenly collapse, crack open, shrivel up, and burn, that wasn't Markie's fault, not really, 'cause if he could've predicted what would happen, which nobody could've, not even Rickabone—(Rickabone could! That's why he *did* it)—he would never in his life, at least not in that way, have made a decision like that. 'Cause now even the doctors are saying they could never have predicted it. (Rickabone could!) That kind of thing never happens. A crack like that right through your body and soul is *temporary*, at least for most people. There are statistics to prove it. No matter how bad they are, those cracks usually mend. So it was

164

more than just grief or desperation or bad luck. It was something in her that was already there."

"Leave me alone."

Michel crawls out of bed, pulls open two hissing cans of beer, and hands one to Jake. Jake drinks and belches.

"A couple of kids," he says. "Don't make me laugh."

"You knew there had to be somebody," says Michel quietly, in the darkness.

"No."

"No idea?"

"Dina used to say it sometimes. It was one way of explaining her acting so strange when she was well, and her, uh, uh, psychosis, later on. I didn't believe it. Still don't, only now I guess I'll have to."

"So now you know it was Markie. What difference does it make? What does it change now that you've got a face, the face of somebody you know, to go along with the accident? The accident's happened, it doesn't matter which streetcar it was."

"Two kids," says Jake bitterly.

"It could just as easily have worked out between those two. For as long as a thing like that lasts, anyway. They really loved each other. Markie loved her, too. They were planning to get married."

"Here's to her old age," says Jake fiercely, high-voiced.

"She was seventeen. Or eighteen. That's the same as twenty-two or -three in your day, you know. Didi couldn't wait to marry Markie. She wanted a big church wedding, she told me so herself."

Then Michel says, more softly, "It was Rickabone. Him alone."

"How?"

"In true Rickabone fashion," says Michel, and betrays his impossible likeness, his inconceivable father. "It was Rickabone who prevented the marriage. We'll never really know why, but if you ask me, it's simple. Rickabone needed money, as usual, a well that could never be filled, and for that reason (lies, lies! The well of evil can never be filled!) and that reason alone, he took Markie, who up until then he'd regarded as his own private property, and signed him over to Salome. He sold Markie to Salome, Jake. And Markie went trotting along, no leash, chain, or muzzle."

"No Didi," says Jake.

"Yes."

It's a long, long time before Jake stretches out and crawls into bed. The bed groans, as usual.

"I'm never going back to the Unicorn again," says Jake.

That morning Michel gives Jake a glass of Seven-Up and three sleeping pills. He waits beside his pillow until Jake drinks it all down.

That morning, and the rest of the day, Rickabone doesn't appear. Jake babbles in his sleep, now and then his voice breaks.

20

"Quit dawdling," says Michel. Jake has been moping around all morning; he doesn't feel like going into town, but he doesn't want to stay in the room, either. He brushes his teeth, for the first time on this trip. He washes his hair, puts on—also for the first time—his good flannel suit with the vest and gray satin tie. His eyes are two slits, the skin around them is puffy and pale pink.

"Don't rush me," he says, furiously rubbing his pointy shoes with the edge of the bedspread.

Michel flops down on the bed.

Jake rummages around in his suitcase and takes out a miniature porcelain soup bowl. On the side of the bowl, painted in pastel tints, is Queen Elizabeth, waving in ermine splendor. A gift for Dina that he bought in London. He picks off the waxed paper and, with the flat handle of the imitation ivory goosefeather that was lying next to the stationery set from the motel, he scoops large globs of pâté out of the bowl. In three minutes he has eaten the whole thing. He licks off the handle and tucks it back between the sheets of airmail stationery. "There," he says, and slides the bulbous little jar under the bed.

Just before they walk out the door Michel undoes the bottom button on Jake's vest.

"If you're going out in your Sunday best, at least do it right."

He loves me, thinks Jake.

"But you sure picked a lousy day to go parading down the Strip."

"What do you mean?" asks Jake, alert, suspicious.

"See for yourself." Michel pulls open the curtains. Shielded by the heavy drapes, bathed in the unearthly light of the red table lamp, caressingly cooled by the air-conditioning, benumbed by the already familiar wheedling and whining of the television commercials, they haven't noticed that a desert wind has risen. "Come on," says Jake.

The grass is flattened. On the surface of the pool is a thick film of grit. Dust swirls into their eyes, their ears. The soda machines rattle as they hurry past, their heads bowed.

Newspapers fly across the boulevard, and rustling tatters of plastic wrap, membranes without fetuses. The multicolored neon lights gleam dully. As Jake and Michel turn the corner, a whirlwind of soot hits them full in the face.

Gasping for breath, they burst into the lobby of Circus Circus. Nothing has changed here, everything's the same, the jingle-jangle of the slot machines, the gambling throng, twisting and turning in the red cocoon.

Michel combs his hair.

Jake's gums are bleeding. "That's what you get for brushing your teeth," he says grumpily.

They shuffle along to the end of a line at the Silver Fountain, where they're each handed a glass of bitter, laboriously bubbling champagne. They toss coins into fruit machines, pull down handles, idly follow the rubbery clattering of the Wheel of Fortune.

168

No chance of serious playing now, they're doomed to lose. Not that they're scared or anything, but there's no point swimming against the current, and what's more—and they both agree about this—they've made a capital error: they didn't bring a large enough bankroll. You should always have a large enough bankroll when you go to Vegas, because no matter what you play, the odds are always against you.

Then Jake strides resolutely, not caring whether Michel is following him or not, to the exhibition. This time he scarcely glances at the curiosa, the instruments, the objects, he just stands and stares at the waxworks, Sankal-Walah, the man who walked around all his life, panting and groaning, with a ton of chains around his neck, a wild-eyed Abraham about to plunge his knife into the shoulder blade of his son Isaac, and, especially, the World's Tallest Man, who gazes down at Jake with an unearthly expression, beyond melancholy or despair, on his pallid face. The polyester is faded, only the eyes still glitter. Yet here in his glass cage, in his dusty brown suit, the World's Tallest Man seems more animated, more alive, than on the TV screen beside him, where you can see him—or rather, a moving monochrome shadow of the man in the cage—trying to fend off a troop of screaming Boy Scouts with wooden hatchets; covering a traffic light with the palm of his hand; in a huge pair of shorts, moving with great, clumsy strides and reluctant joints among frenzied, dwarflike basketball players and placing a ball, like a precious jewel, in the net in front of his nose.

"He died at the age of thirty-two," Michel reads aloud from the card. "And he kept on growing, right up to the very last day."

Jake buys a color photo of the Tallest Man in the World.

"For Didi?"

"For me," says Jake, bashful, grim. "And for Dina. She'll be happy to know there are even stranger people on this earth than me." He clasps the photo under his arm, then slips it under his vest.

As they work their way through fried chicken and tough, recycled potatoes, Jake more ravenously than ever, a shaven youth in saffron-colored robes wanders over to their table and lays a paper rose next to Jake's plate. Then he waits, looking sheepish.

"Leave me alone," says Jake, his mouth full of potato.

The youth takes back the flower. Tears trickle out of Jake's narrowed eyes, glimmer on the swollen lids, on his soot-speckled nose.

"I have to go home," he says.

Michel calls over the waitress.

"No, I mean *home* home," says Jake, and wipes his eyes on a mustard-stained napkin, then gasps, swears.

A taxi drives them downtown in a cloud of swirling grit. "Where're you from?" asks the black man behind the wheel.

"From the moon," says Jake. The taxi driver rocks back and forth over his steering wheel, hiccuping with laughter. "That's a good one," he says. "Man, that's a good one. I know just how you feel!"

In a huge movie theater, the walls of which are adorned with Grecian columns, sphinxes, and lotus blossoms, and which seems to be filled almost exclusively with Mexicans and blacks, they see *Pussy Love*, a plotless story about high school girls getting chained to radiators, pimply kids jerking themselves off, fingers foraging in an asshole. The images flicker, the camera focuses on a painting, on a lamp, pans a naked, pink tangle of bodies on a Persian rug, a vibrator trembles across a shaven cunt. Jake gets up.

"This was a bad idea," he says at the exit, where more blacks and Mexicans are hanging around. For a moment Michel is afraid that he and Jake have been spotted and that the bastards are now plotting how to finish off this pair of White Devils once and for all. He checks with his elbow to make sure he's got his *Hitler-jugend* dagger, but the men just stand there, smoking, dreaming, chewing, waiting.

In the bar next door to the movie theater they order double whiskeys, which is something else they'll be sure and tell 'em back at the Unicorn: how stingy these American barkeepers are with the booze.

"What you said before about Rickabone," says Jake, "about him needing money, I can imagine that. When he needed money he wouldn't stop at anything, that Rickabone. I don't know how many times he called me up at three in the morning. 'Jake, I'm here in Ostend, do me a favor and drive over to Doctor Groot-jan's house on the double, without delay, and drive him up here in your car, he'll know what it's about,' and then Doctor Grootjans would bring him fifty, eighty, a hundred thousand francs, and if it was a hundred thousand Rickabone would sign a check for a hundred fifty thousand. Or else it was: 'Jake, I'm calling from the casino in Blankenburghe, drive right over here and bring Juliette and Leon and Staf van 't Peperstraatje, they'll know what it's about, they're waiting for you at the Unicorn, and make it snappy, because they're trying to close up here and this time I'm going to rub their noses in the rules and regulations, those Blankenburghe bumpkins,' and while His Lordship'd be standing around at the roulette table in the empty hall drinking one espresso after the other, the four of us would have to play at the other tables, for hours—with *twenty-franc chips!* we might as well have been using bottlecaps—'cause as long as there are five customers they're not allowed to close for the night. No, he wouldn't stop at anything, you never knew what he was going to do next. How much was it he inherited from Pa Bone? Twenty million francs. How long did it take him to get through that twenty million? A year and a half. A Panhard, a Maserati, twelve new suits in one afternoon, I was there, every night at the Parisiana, with all those French girls they got there, girls *and* boys, just the way he liked it, champagne for everyone, and every day of the week at the Unicorn with his two attaché cases, one for his pills and the other for his thousand-franc notes, his ammo, he always called it.

"Of course he needed money, the way he used to fill up all the numbers on the roulette board, over four or five tables, like confetti, and then if he heard the croupier call out: Seventeen! he was the happiest man in Belgium, but in order to win twenty thousand on seventeen, he'd gambled away fifty.

"Of course he needed money, him more than any of us. I even loaned him some. Six thousand francs. He wanted to write a check for ten thousand. He was holding his checkbook, you remember how he was at the end, couldn't even write his own name anymore, after three letters his arm dropped and there'd be this long streak of ink, you had to hold his hand steady. 'Right, ten thousand, eh, Jacob?' I told him: 'No, Mister Bone, six thousand. And not one franc more. I'm not like that.' 'Jackass,' he said, and that was it."

The umpteenth litany of Rickabone. Nostalgic, reverential. Not a trace of bitterness or envy. It's a fucking catharsis, thinks Michel as they start on their third double whiskey. Just look at Jake, the mere memory of Rickabone is enough to reconcile him to the situation. Look, he's actually smiling at the bleary mob stumbling out of the movie theater into the harsh white light.

Outside, in the busy shopping street, the storm has died down. Jake and Michel cross at an intersection, dodging the passing cars to reach a slowly approaching cab, when suddenly, out of thin air, a policeman looms up and blocks their way. A slight, blond young man with a glittering badge. The lower half of his face is twitching from side to side. They can't understand him over the din of the traffic, but then Michel realizes he's just chewing a piece of gum. The clear, childishly arrogant gaze settles first on Michel, then shifts to Jake. The cop takes a step forward—he comes up to Jake's shoulder—and jabs his black leather forefinger into Jake's belly. "Would you mind stepping back, sir?"

Jake does what he says, then turns to Michel, dumbfounded.

"Fine. Now, would you mind remaining on the sidewalk until I say you can get off it?"

The cop turns his back to them. The monstrous, gleaming cars race past; slowly exploding rockets of neon light ripple across their flanks.

Michel can see, can feel Jake's helpless rage. Jake is gasping for breath, he longs to hurl himself at the cop with the full weight of his bisontine body and send him flying against the hood of a car. But his shoulders sag, and once again his overwhelmingly lonely sorrow triumphs over that other, sharper, deeper humiliation. Jake takes two, three faltering steps in the other direction and breaks into a run down a filthy, unlit side street. Michel catches up with him just as he's slowing down.

"I'm hungry," says Jake. "Are you?"

"I thought you'd never ask," lies Michel.

Noel's Place. A bare, cheerless room, wooden benches, a wall lined with vending machines. Blacks in white aprons clear away plates and cups. Seven or eight men are sitting around the room, staring into space. The fluorescent lights on the ceiling shine like the sun in a frozen sky. Michel buys hot dogs, pastrami sandwiches, four cans of Schlitz Malt.

"You," says Jake, "you were talking to me today while I was

asleep, back in our room. Don't think I'm so stupid that I didn't feel it. You said a whole lot of things to my face while I was sleeping, things maybe you thought would make me mad. Don't look at me like that, Michel. Admit it. For once in your life."

"I slept the whole day. Like you."

"I heard you," says Jake. "What kind of a jerk do you think I am?"

"So what did I say?"

"That I wasn't a real man. That the reason Dina's so sad is because she doesn't screw every day of the week, that she's off fooling around with other guys now that she's got the chance. You were talking very softly. You said Markie van Schechem was more of a man than I was. 'Cause otherwise there's no way of explaining why Didi went out with him."

Michel gets two more cans of beer. Not American this time, but Japanese. Kirin, it's called. Made from rice and hops.

Jake says, "Don't try and deny it, Michel. It's not worth the trouble."

He pulls the photo of the World's Tallest Man out from under his vest, looks at it, drains his glass, rips the photo into jagged squares, and piles them into the ashtray. Next to Michel's foot is a stain, dark and dry, blood and puke, shaped like a fat little bird with tiny wings.

Outside, the night is filled with noises, transistors playing rock music, drums from a nearby nightclub, singing, shouting, cars honking in Morse code, three short honks and two long, the laughter of young girls.

Four young men walk into Noel's Place dressed in silver jackets, vinyl bell-bottoms, silk scarves, gold bracelets. Their delicate, pointy faces are powdered white, and two of them have painted bright blue shadows under their cheekbones. Giggling, exuberant, they flip open the doors of the vending machines. The youngest is wearing earrings. With his almond-shaped eyes, false lashes, and full red lips, whose contours are accentuated by a dark red line, he looks like that Roman emperor on TV a few weeks before who was so stark raving mad he put his horse on the throne. The boy stands apart from the others, as if he wants nothing to do with them, his glittering, twittering peers. He looks at Jake. Jake doesn't notice. He's drying his eyes on his sleeve.

"In the beginning," says Jake in his high, tentative voice, "when I saw Didi was never going to get well again, I started losing my hair, great big hunks of it."

A couple of the dancers are playing a game in which they each hold out a fist, two outstretched fingers, or an upturned palm. They bubble with laughter. Gold dust glitters in their sculpted curls and on their eyelids.

"They must be dancers from a show," says Michel.

"No, they're from Circus Circus," says Jake. "I saw them dancing on the big ladder. Up and down."

Why is the discontented youngest, the one with the peachiest skin, staring so obstinately at Jake?

"Looks like you've got another admirer," says Michel.

"Me?"

"Yes, that one over there." (The one with the defenseless, impressionable charm of Markie van Schechem. But I'll keep that to myself.)

Jake meets his eyes, two precious stones, opaline ovals, with pupils of aquamarine, set in thick, jet-black lashes. Michel sees the blood draining from Jake's face; in the icy light the furrows along his nose and the bags under his eyes are black as soot, like a black-and-white photograph.

"You want Japanese beer or American?" asks Michel, who is suddenly having trouble swallowing.

Jake shoves away the table.

"Stay here," hisses Michel. Jake doesn't hear him. He moves, like a sleepwalker, past the tables, past an old gentleman holding his newspaper two inches away from his nose, past the long row of vending machines, until he reaches the dancer, who hasn't taken his eyes off him for a moment. Then Michel, riveted to his seat, hears Jake ask, "Who are you? What's your name?"

The expression on the boy's face doesn't change. Next to him the finger game stops; one of the players is left holding out two ridiculously widespread fingers, like a pair of scissors.

Jake's voice breaks. "Tell me your name! I've got to know who you are!"

"Why don't you just tell him, angel?" asks a dancer sitting against the wall with his knees raised.

The young man shakes his head. With a sudden, decisive movement, that seems to go on forever, Jake's hands reach out and seize the dancer by the throat. He lifts the boy up by the neck, up off the bench. Before the thrashing, sparkling silver arms can get a grip on Jake's Sunday best, the white-powdered face is suspended in midair, terror-stricken, a foot above Jake's own head. One, two, three seconds. Then Jake brings down the head of curls against the metal edge of a vending machine, with a crash like the echo of an ax in a tree, deep in a forest. The jacket makes a ripping sound as the boy crumples, knees splayed. His chin hits the floor. The curls drip, glistening crimson.

One of the dancers shrieks like a girl. Without looking back, almost indifferently, Jake walks out the door. Michel sees his shadow bobbing across the frosted windowpane. He jumps up, hurries past the chirping dancers, who have swooped down on the motionless, irreparably damaged boy, past an old, trembling black waiter who threatens him with a carving fork.

Michel runs all the way to the other end of Noel's Place, finds himself in a hot haze of cooking fumes, niggers scream behind sizzling stoves, he reaches an alleyway, bangs his hip against a pile of crates, pulls out his dagger, panting, but no one comes after him, he makes his way back to the bustling, noisy street, where country music twangs from the loudspeakers of toy stores, TV stores, jeans stores, and leaps into a taxi, just as it's screeching to a halt.

21

THE FIRST FIVE MINUTES back in their motel room Michel packs his things in a panic. Then he starts talking to himself and calms down. Slowly, methodically, he folds up pants and shirts, arranges them in his suitcase. "The toilet stuff, we leave here," he says, "for the next victim."

"Idiot," says Rickabone.

"Keep quiet," says Michel.

Now and then he listens at the door.

Feet up on the glass coffee table, he leafs through *Penthouse*.

"Yes, gentlemen, the man answering to the name of Jake or Jacob is my friend," he says, like a witness on *Perry Mason*. "And yes, I am, in a sense, an accomplice, but, gentlemen of the jury, my friend and brother was provoked, he was a victim of indecent assault. What would you do, you pioneers, you full-blooded American men, how would you react if such a loathesome pervert were to cast doubt on your manliness?"

"Bastard," says Rickabone.

"No more of a bastard than you are," says Michel.

"Alas, my dear boy, that's true. No more of a bastard than I am. And you never will be."

178

Michel watches "The Late Late Show," and countless, identical commercials in which happy homemakers sing the praises of dishwashing liquid. Around four in the morning he leaves the door ajar and sets out for Circus Circus. He searches for Jake among the swarms of players, marks keno tickets, wins forty dollars, drinks watery whiskey at the bar, where preteen hookers are waiting for business. Finally they set up the boxing ring and the kangaroo appears, to feeble applause and a ruffle of drums.

While the (fully recovered?) creature flings its paws around the neck of a fat girl in a tutu, presses its belly against her, and shakes, Amos, in livery, stands outside the ring and pleads with the snickering spectators. "Let's have a really big hand for our daring young Lucy! Come on, ladies and gentlemen, you can do better than that!" When Michel goes up to him, Amos says, pointing, "Over there. Second door on the right. He's in bad shape. Wait for me. If anybody asks, just tell them you two are from the Council of European Churches."

In a large storeroom, among colorful balloons, aluminum ladders, hoops, collapsible metal tables, and two cages of white doves, is Jake, slumped in a flabby heap, sound asleep, with a child-size pair of sunglasses on his nose. He looks pinker and fatter than ever, yet when he sits up, his movements are confused, impaired.

"We've got to get out of here," says Michel.

"Are you mad at me?" Even the high voice has something impaired about it.

"I knew when we left that you'd get me in trouble," says Michel, but it doesn't sound like a reproach. "What does Amos say about it?"

"That we should get the hell out of Las Vegas. Over the

179

Nevada border. That they've probably got all the bus stations and airports under police, uh, surveillance."

"Amos can suck my dick," says Michel.

Thunderous applause. Has Lucy flattened the kangaroo?

Jake says, "Amos heard about it over the radio. He's got a skull base fracture and he's not going to make it."

When Amos appears he has changed out of his circus garb into a white jean suit with epaulettes. At the end of his legs, which look more spindly than ever, is a huge pair of cowboy boots. He sits down on a bucket. "Now listen," he says. "I've done what I could. You can leave within three-quarters of an hour. A good friend of mine'll take care of everything. He's got a Convair 240." He hands Jake a roll of candy. The giant chews, rubs his eyes. There's a chink of light falling through the door that keeps changing color, from red to blue to green to yellow.

"Thank you, my friend," says Jake.

"I'm on," says Amos. "Come back soon. I'll show you my mulberry garden."

"It's a promise," says Jake. "And when we do, we'll definitely bring a bigger bankroll."

"The knife thrower awaits me!" says Amos importantly. With the elegant verve of a circus star, with nothing to remind you of the dealer's rigidity or the preacher's wrath, he leaps up from his bucket, claps Jake on the shoulder, and disappears. He hasn't so much as glanced at Michel the entire time.

The airport lies in the middle of the desert like a summer resort, with abundant greenery and rock 'n' roll music. At the bar, which also serves as a check-in counter, are some twenty passengers, including a busily gesticulating, giggly group in red velvet caps shaped like truncated cones, with gold tufts and gold cuneiform script.

"Sonofabitch," hisses Jake, turning abruptly. As if the back of him isn't just as suspicious as the front, thinks Michel.

"What's wrong?" But Michel has already guessed the reason for Jake's fear. Three close-cropped young men in black suits, silent, unsmiling, disquietingly calm, are waiting by the glass door, through which you can see the plane. All three have black leather attaché cases, and one of them is carrying a tennis racket.

"Keep calm," says Michel. He drinks an ice-cold beer at the bar. Jake doesn't want anything. His tight-lipped face is that of a stranger. The cigarette in his mouth is unlit. The sun shines through his big pink ears, delicately veined, like a rose. (I couldn't help him even if I wanted to. I'll dream about this some day, the heat, the bulbous, two-engine plane that must be at least thirty years old, the propellers are already turning. Throughout my life I'll have seen everything with remote control, one touch of the button and another channel flops onto my lens, with different colors, different scenery, stranger apparitions.)

"Amos is a real friend," says Jake.

"And I'm not?"

"You're not," says Jake. "You're different."

"What do you mean, different?"

Jake shrugs his shoulders, knits his brow.

"Amos is more of a friend like Rev'em-up Red," he says. "Somebody who'd do a pal a favor without even being asked. There aren't many like that. You know why he doesn't want to raise cattle on his ranch? 'Cause when he was a kid his parents had cattle and they had to stand around in the desert for so long they were covered with dust, and with all the sun and rain and dust they started growing grass on their hides. He couldn't stand the sight, he told me."

A policeman in a short-sleeved khaki shirt walks up to them.

"You the guys from Circus Circus?" asks the cop, a white-haired fellow with an impudent grin.

Michel, his mouth gone dry, says, "We've got reservations."

"You carrying firearms of any kind?"

"No," say Jake and Michel, in chorus.

"Hmmm," says the cop. Looking Michel up and down with the cool, detached gaze of a doctor, he grabs hold of his walkie-talkie and says, "Yes?" He nods. "Yes. One-o-nine-o. Right on. Bye."

"Eigenschwiller!" shouts one of the unsmiling young men at the glass door. The cop swings around. The young man points to his watch. "Three minutes," says the cop, holding up three fingers.

Jake and Michel have to state their names. The cop plucks one of the five ballpoints from his breast pocket and takes down their names on a dog-eared memo pad.

"Amos better watch out," he says. "One of these days he's gonna be up shit's creek."

He sticks the memo pad back in his pocket and says, "Okay, let's move. Follow me." He walks toward the glass door. Turns out he's the pilot of the Convair. They follow him across the cracked cement.

In the half-empty plane Jake refuses to sit next to Michel.

"Do I smell or something?"

"No. I just gotta think."

"Okay, boy," says Michel.

When they're in the air Michel turns around and looks at him. Jake raises his eyebrows three times; the tiny sunglasses bounce up and down. He clings to the seat in front of him, his face ashen.

"You okay?"

"Yes."

"There's a restroom at the back."

"I'll wait. Michel!"

"Yes?"

"Did you insure us?"

"No."

"Oh, great."

One of the unsmiling young men, who is sitting in front of Michel next to a man in a fez, says, "Brother, I've been a Shriner since I was sixteen. And it's the best thing that ever happened to me in my whole life. Where did you stay, brother?"

"At the Flamingo, brother."

"And did you win, brother?"

"I was attending a pyramidology conference," the man replies tartly.

Past the mountains. The rose-hued, improbable mountains. The engines sputter.

22

"**WHAT DO WE DO NOW?**" says Michel in their motel room. For the hundredth and final time.

"It's up to you."

The room has a view of the turquoise-tiled swimming pool, around which are plaster statues of Venus and David and a bunch of bare-assed Greeks. The walls of their room are ocher stucco, cracked here and there. The chairs have plastic cane seats. Next to the gilt-edged mirrors are bronze torches with flame-shaped lightbulbs. Ebony night tables, nine-sided, too many sided, too close to the bed. Even the ashtrays are black with nine sides.

"What do we do now? I asked you first, you have to answer."

"No movies," says Jake. "No porn movies, no funny movies, no sad movies, no action movies."

At the reception desk they change their last Belgian francs. Whatever happens, they're not going to do anything crazy with it, they've made up their minds.

Besides, what's a gambling joint around here anyway? An ordinary building in the middle of a row of houses. You might as well go to the casino in Blankenburghe. What am I saying? You'd be better off in Blankenburghe!

Out on the street, in a city that suddenly seems very European, without a single towering silver spike heel glittering in the sun or whispering through the night with a thousand neon lights, Jake and Michel walk very close together, as if they have been caught up in a cycle of normalcy, of families, monthly wages, promotions, overtime. They miss that sand castle in the middle of the desert, sheltered by the ring of sea-blue and rose-colored mountains, something that now lies behind them, a gash of light in the pale Los Angeles sky.

They drink coffee. Two cups of light brown, transparent, scalding liquid. "Horse piss," says Jake.

What next? "We should send postcards before it's too late."

"It's already too late. We'll get there before they do," says Michel.

"I should've sent one to my father," Jake sighs. "A card would've made him so happy. He just sits around all day in that home. He can hardly see anymore, but he can see well enough for a postcard from America. All he ever does is eat. He eats everything in sight. Whole boxes of cookies."

"Sounds like you."

"No!" cries Jake. "It's not the same. I eat out of nerves."

Jake's probably a good father to Didi, thinks Michel. Kind, patient, eager to please. But does he have anything to teach his child? Anything to hold up as an example? (Thank God I'll never play that role, never have to. Does that mean I'm just living for myself? Yes, for whatever may come, doesn't matter what. But I'm paying the price. The highest price. With my phantom, my fantasy of Rickabone. Rickabone is not something I want. Something inside of me wants him, in spite of myself, like a craving for cigarettes, or a hard-on.)

They walk past the stores. What've they got here that you can't get back home?

"Those beans in red sauce," says Jake, and buys a dozen cans at the supermarket, as well as a porcelain whiskey bottle shaped like a miniature motorcycle.

"For Rev'em-up Red," he says. "His eyes'll pop out when he sees this!"

It's true. Every night Rev'em-up Red parks his motorcycle next to his bed. He always carries around a little jar of enamel paint to touch up any unexpected scratches. The first time Michel rode on the back of his Yamaha he swore he'd never do it again. He was terrified! 'Cause at every intersection on Veldstraat, Rev made that thing rear up, the front wheel leaped into the air like the front legs of a horse, and on the highway he overtook a BMW at a hundred miles an hour, slowed down, drove right up alongside the BMW, pulled the gauge out of his oil tank and, snickering at the driver, he slowly, provocatively licked the gleaming black needle. Sometimes Rev'em-up Red's whole bedroom shakes with the roar of engines coming from four loudspeakers, while motor oil sizzles on a gas burner, filling the air with its fumes.

Jake weighs the porcelain motorcycle in his hand.

"This'll sure make him happy," he says. "But it's too heavy."

He screws off the cap and drains the contents in three gulps, then shudders, his jowls wobbling.

"Jesus, this tastes like something out of a sewer."

In the party goods department he buys a rubber Nixon mask. "I can't wait to walk into the Unicorn wearing this."

"I thought you were never going back there."

"You're right," he says quietly, suddenly somber.

In the window of a jewelry shop sits a plump little woman dressed as a nurse, prying open an oyster with a kitchen knife and then quickly, mechanically, chopping it up. Her red sausage fingers in their skins of transparent glove remove a magnificent, flawless pearl and hold it up to the light. Then she presents the pearl to one of the jostling customers.

"Think Dina'd like one of those?" asks Jake.

"Think she'd know the difference between a pearl like that and one from the Grand Bazar?"

(That sounded more contemptuous than I meant it to.)

"No."

The round little nurse is hacking away at a new oyster.

"It's really kind of a shame, though," says Jake. "Chopping up all those nice oysters like that. It's murder."

"What did you say?"

Jake freezes. "You're right. I clean forgot."

(Now that the word is out, hanging in the air between us, it's got meaning. For Jake it means something concrete, complete, terrible. For me too. Must be contagious.)

A few streets down Jake says, "It was an accident."

The air smells vaguely of gas.

"What's the difference between here and our Veldstraat?" says Jake. "Huh? I mean, they've got the same clothes, same jeans, same music in all the stores, same old movies in the movie theaters, the Burger Kings are the same, the hairdressers, the cars . . ."

(He can't tell the difference. Not any more. I see it less and less myself. The difference between us and the real travelers. Real travelers immerse themselves in a foreign land, in foreignness, they sink into it, lose themselves in it, blushing with local color. We're tourists, nothing more, always on the lookout for something strange, something spicy we can tell 'em back at the Unicorn, or Jake can tell Dina, and I, my mother.)

"These days everybody knows everything about everywhere and everybody and they're always copying everybody else," says Jake.

In Chinatown he points to a blue-and-red-checked wool shirt on a dummy of a hefty, platinum-blond lumberjack.

"Think I'd look good in that?" asks Jake in a hesitant, humble little voice.

"It's just your style," says Michel.

"Or is it more for winter?"

"You think it's never going to be winter again?"

In a cramped space bulging with jeans, sweaters, and jackets, under a glaring light, Jake tries on the shirt. An old Chinese man tugs it down over Jake's belly.

"Fits like a glove," says Michel.

"You can say that again. I can't breathe."

Michel asks for a larger size.

"This is jumbo size," says the old man.

"King size," corrects his son.

"He need emperor size," says the father, giggling.

"You tryin' to bust my balls?" snarls Jake. Startled by the tone of his voice, the two salesmen quickly squeeze him into a red-and-white-checked cotton shirt. Jake, bright red and reeking of sweat, holds in his stomach; the buttons are about to pop. "Good, fine," he says hurriedly.

"It stretch," says the old, emaciated Chinaman.

"It's the kind of material that stretches in the wash," says the son.

In a restaurant with walls of lacquered ox-blood, they eat meat, fish, chicken, shrimp, spareribs, and squid, with bowls of Cantonese rice and dishes of sweet-and-sour sauce and four pints of Chinese beer each. Twenty-four bucks, that's cheaper than in Vlaanderenstraat. Coffee and oily, sweet liqueur.

They break open their fortune cookies and pull out the paper strips.

"'The burden that you must bear is great, yet your heart pounds at the challenge,'" Michel reads aloud.

"I don't get it," says Jake. He stares down at his own fortune for a moment.

"Give it to me. I'll translate." Jake pushes away his hand.

"No," he says, "I mean, I don't get how they can say it so well. It's like those Chinese can look right into my brain. 'I willingly' . . . willingly?"

"Gladly," says Michel.

"' . . . accept love's a-*go*-ny,' I gladly accept love's a-*go*-ny. HuShih. In nineteen hundred and nineteen."

"*A*-gony. That means unbearable pain, torment."

"I know that!" cries Jake.

The Chinese waiter is still standing at their table. He looks angry. What's the problem? He says that the tip, a dollar, isn't enough.

"Here," says Jake, handing him three dollars. "For you, sir, willingly!"

Outside, at a pushcart, he buys a huge white cotton candy. He's still biting into the fluff as they stand in the doorway of a temple watching a bespectacled Chinaman in mandarin garb painting flowers. Leaning over the paper, he dips the nail of his little finger, which has been filed to a point, into the ink and sweeps an exceedingly delicate and graceful line across the thirsty paper, then two more fine lines, and there appears, before their astonished eyes, a branch with twigs and leaves. Then the dark, curved, weathered middle finger brushes the surface of a red ink tray and, in the same elegant motion, the empty space beside a twig—and there's a perfect cherry hanging on the page.

"Goddamn," says Jake, awestruck. "Out of nowhere. If you can do that . . ." He licks off his cotton candy stick and slips it in his

189

breast pocket. He buys the cherry, and the Mandarin stamps his name on it. "Chung Soon," he says to Jake. "That means: Honesty." He rolls it up and slides it between the cans of beans and the porcelain motorcycle in Jake's plastic shopping bag.

"Mister Honesty," says Jake, "you're the greatest artist I've ever seen."

"Yes," says the man, with dignity. "Even in Canada."

"My daughter paints, too. But with crayons."

"My uncle paints with his tongue. On Fourteenth Street," says the Mandarin, as his precise, careful fingers arrange a new sheet of paper.

"That doesn't sound very healthy," says Jake. "Well, Mister Honesty, all the best." He tries to shake the Mandarin's hand, but the man buries it in his wide, spattered, silk sleeve and bows low.

It's getting darker. But only up there, above the rooftops.

A blond whore in raincoat and boots, with a twirling orange umbrella on her shoulder, says, "Hi, Fatso."

"He's the one you want," says Jake, pointing to Michel. "He's ready to explode."

She laughs at Michel. "I live right around the corner."

"Aren't you scared of me?"

"No. Should I be?"

"I'm the Paradise Strangler," says Michel. "The olive-colored one, can't you tell?"

The many-pointed star stops turning.

"No kidding!"

They walk on.

"That pigsweat I bought for Rev 'em-up Red is fogging up my head," says Jake.

In the drugstore he has trouble working the coffee machine.

"You have to pull the handle right down, fast, the American

way," says Michel. The giant tugs at the handle, the metal monster shakes from top to bottom and nearly topples over. "Nonono," says a broadly smiling Japanese gentleman in a striped suit, and points upward. Jake, his face twisted with hate and shame, pushes up the handle and brings the two cups of coffee over to their table.

"There's only one thing that matters to you," he says. "Laughing at me. Putting me down. Making me look stupid in front of one of those yellow monkeys. That's the only reason you asked me to come here in the first place, isn't it?"

"You really believe that?"

"No," says Jake. He drinks. "Horse piss," he decides.

At the table next to them, an elegant mulatto is holding his newspaper two inches away from his glasses (like an old gentleman next to a vending machine under a frosty sun). At his elbow, half-hidden by the newspaper, a miniature television murmurs.

"Our last night," says Jake absently.

"If you still want to buy a present for Dina you better do it now."

"You're right. You're a real pal."

In a comfortably cool lingerie shop Jake buys a short black see-through nightie with purple ribbons. The two young salesgirls are only too eager to help. Jake holds the nightie up to the light. The seriousness with which he examines the flimsy stuff between his thick fingers provokes tinkling, smothered giggles from the girls.

"What d'you think?" asks Jake. Michel hesitates. "Maybe."

"If it's meant for the gentleman, I'd suggest a smaller size," says one of the salesgirls graciously. The other one spins around and buries her face in a boa.

Jake flushes scarlet. "No, miss," he mumbles. "No," he says, as he pays for the nightie, "no, it's a present for my wife."

As she rings up the sale he stands there rubbing his eyes, which are fiery red and damp.

"There's an eyelash in my eye," he says, taking out a handkerchief and starting for the door.

"Wait!" cries the salesgirl. It's an order. Jake stiffens. "You forgot your receipt," she says, smiling sweetly.

Outside he blows his nose loudly. "What with that weather and this cotton shirt, I must've caught a cold. I could sure use a drink."

In a dark, crowded bar he turns his glass of whiskey around and around in his hand, suspiciously. "They throw in some kind of drug," he says, "and it knocks you out and you wake up with your face in a garbage can, with no money or passport, with no shoes on. That's the way they are around here."

The jukebox is playing "Puppy Love." The blacks at the bar have loud, hoarse, cheerful voices, they nudge each other and laugh, not a care in the world.

"Michel," says the dejected, thin, white voice, "you can tell me now, we're pals and it's our last day, why did you bring me here with you?"

"Because I wanted to win. A beginner is always lucky at cards. And I wanted to hitch a ride on your wagon." (I'm lying again. I can't help it. One of these days it'll hit me, like a dazzling light, the Truth, unvarnished, indisputable, in all its ramifications.) ("Idiot," says Rickabone.)

"A beginner? Me? I've gambled away fortunes in my life!" ("Fortunes!" hiccups Rickabone.)

"Yes," says Michel. "No. Not a beginner. You're more of an innocent bystander."

"Thanks," says Jake. "It's real decent of you that you have the nerve to admit it. Thanks."

They both get drunk. "Those niggers," says Jake, "they've all got razors on 'em. That one for sure." He nods toward a tall, very black man with pale scars on his cheeks. "Later on, when there's a full moon, he'll hit the streets. He's got to have his first victim before tomorrow morning. Doesn't matter who it is. As long as he's white. Slit his throat right open. Swish, swish. No mercy. Willingly."

"I'm sure he'd love to get his hands on you. With all those nice, juicy layers of bacon."

"Yes," says Jake, thoughtfully rubbing his loins, his belly. "That would sure make his night."

Out on the street he tosses five dollars into the tambourine of a pale, freckled little girl singing, "Hallelujah, praise the Lord!"

As he walks he looks up timidly at the soaring skyscrapers with their myriad lit windows. "Wouldn't be too hard from up there," he says, "with a good pair of sights on your long rifle." He tears open his jacket, waves the plastic shopping bag, and howls to the skies, "Hey! Here he is!" He points to a bulging white spot above his navel, where a button has popped.

"Here! Ready! Aim! Fire!" Michel pulls him along. "Willingly!" bellows Jake.

They trudge on, down wider, deserted streets. Jake drops heavily onto the edge of a concrete planter outside a bank. Next to him, geraniums are growing in damp ocher soil.

"Willingly."

"Come on back to the motel," says Michel. "We'll play some cards and go to bed. Wake up feeling nice and fit. We've got to leave at eleven, at the latest." (Jesus, I sound like a meddlesome old aunt.)

"Willingly." He doesn't budge.

(The flabby king among the flowers. His innocence is genuine, but idiotic. Idiotic as the world itself. The cumbrous reality of him, the inertia, is unbearable, and there's nothing to relieve the burden, no echo, no reflection, a truth without a key.)

Stifling an acid belch, Michel spits out, "Get up, you stupid fuck! That goddamn bawling of yours the whole time . . ."

"You shouldn't say that." Jake gets up halfway and holds out his hand, as if to caress him, but Michel turns around and marches down a side street, expecting to hear a shout, or a pitiful cry, but all he hears is the hum of the restless city.

23

JAKE TAKES A BUS. And another one. The sea murmurs. Santa Monica? Road signs. Malibu. No, no.

It was just around the corner. Or was it? Is anything ever just around the corner in this sprawling city? Palm trees sway as he walks by. He stammers something to a taxi driver. The taxi cruises for three quarters of an hour past mansions and tree-lined avenues.

"Hollywood," says Jake.

"This is Hollywood," says the driver. "The Boulevard!"

"This is the Boulevard."

"It's goddamn simple, asshole, Hollywood Boulevard, where the action is!"

Jake recognizes toy stores, a supermarket. "Stop!"

The driver plucks a couple of dollars from Jake's fist, taps his forehead. "Good luck!"

At one of the newsstands that sells newspapers from around the world, Jake, cackling with delight, finds a *Zondagskrant* from three weeks before. The paper is clammy. The letters on the page tell him all kinds of interesting things. The truth about Miss

World. Grayish photographs. When Jennifer Hosten won the title, her native Grenada was so ecstatic they issued a special stamp in her honor. Professor discovers why some people have such trouble sleeping. Rita Hayworth suffers nervous breakdown. John Lennon says: Music is like a microbe.

Jake stows the paper away in his shopping bag. Searches. Recognizes a movie theater with a pagoda roof. Wasn't this where people pressed their hands and feet in cement?

(I can't take another step. I'm too heavy. This heart, *my* heart, is drowning in fat. The fat is choking me. The veins in my legs, there was something wrong with them, too, Doctor Verbraeken said. Dry mouth. Tongue like a crust of bread. Where was it? I can't go on.)

Jake drags his feet all the way to the end of the Boulevard. Then all the way back, on the opposite side of the street. And then suddenly, hoped-for, yet barely believed, he sees them. He rubs his burning eyes, his heart throbs in his parched mouth. There they stand, the boys, *her* boys, pimply and arrogant, next to their motorcycles. *Aryans*, he reads on the leather back of a boy who has fallen asleep against his bike, head nodding on the thin neck, a fallen, broken angel. Jake shuffles closer and stands before them, wanting nothing more than to drop to his knees and lie down in the shadow of the nearest housefront, but that's not why he has come, why he's come back after all this time. The sun is high in the sky, the air is like powder, where is she?

"Hi, man!" says Jake. He hears his own voice, foolish, desperate.

"Hey," says a foxlike face. "If you wanna score, you're on the wrong track." (I'm too tired. I can't understand English anymore. Why don't they just talk like me?)

"Fuck off, man." (That, I understand. But I'm not leaving. No way. I've got a right to be on the Boulevard. Where is she? Their leader, the one with the shaved eyebrows, isn't here either. He had reddish, slicked-back hair. Isn't that true, Michel? I remember more than you think, traitor.)

With the round, hard, lumpy bundle of plastic in his arms and against his cheek, he sits down, aching feet in the gutter and butt on the sidewalk, just inches away from the passersby, who look down on him, want something from him.

(The Aryans are snickering. They're pointing at me, at my bare, white belly. Three—wait, I'll count them, one, two, three, four buttons have popped, the buttonholes are torn. My brand-new shirt. Fit me like a glove, the traitor said.)

"Hey, what're ya doing'? Askin' me to dance?" says a fourteen-year-old Aryan.

"Willingly."

"Ooooh! The Force is with him!" the kid hoots.

They shriek with laughter. (Where is that woman? She's the only thing that's happened to me in America, the only thing that *can* happen to me. What else did he say, the traitor? That only eleven percent of the crimes in California ever get solved. The Aryans think I'm a waste of time, or they would've ripped open my pockets by now with their knives, stolen all my money and my passport. I can't keep my eyes open.)

He wakes up—the sun is beating down brighter than ever, the Boulevard screams with car horns and sirens—and sees her making a call from a phone booth. No, she's gone into the booth, grubbed around in the coin slot, and disappeared.

Jake grabs his plastic shopping bag and runs, the shiny white bulge clutched to his belly, into the side street. A ruttish, hot wave

of joy washes over his eyes when he sees her, leaning against a cigarette machine in the blazing sun. She's wearing a fur jacket that
comes down to her hips. Where's the army blanket that en-
veloped her like a cape? He comes closer. Around her neck is
the dog collar with the brass studs (that kept flashing into his
mind all the time he was in that distant desert city), along the
side of her nose is a wide pink stripe that looks as if it's been
drawn on with crayon. His heart pounds; he's so tired. The clear
whites of her eyes between the multicolored lashes. She doesn't
recognize him.

"It's me."

"Hi, doll," she says, and that familiar voice, ravaged by whiskey
and sorrow, fills him with joy.

Can he spare a dollar?

"Dollars, as many as you want," he says.

"Then give me twenty."

"Okay, Rachel."

"Hey, you know me?" (How could I not know you, how could
I not recognize those perfect teeth, that girlish laugh!)

"Are you an old lover of mine?" (I understand every syllable of
her unfathomable, American voice.)

"Yes," says Jake. "You remember, don't you?"

"Sure."

"I'm from Belgium. Don't you remember?"

"If you give me twenty bucks, I'll suck the hell out of you."

"The hell?"

"The hell, sweetie."

He puts down the heavy plastic bag, pulls a wad of dollar bills
out of his pants pocket, pushes away her eager hand, and holds
the green, crumpled wad under her nose. "Here, you can smell it,
sweetie."

"Right this way." She grabs hold of his arm.

She's much shorter than he is, and slighter than he remembers. Shuffling along beside her, towering above her, he feels like a cumbersome ogre being led through the impenetrable, immeasurable forest by Little Red Riding Hood. Her piercing gaze is fixed straight ahead. She has small, dainty ears.

She stops at a Pepsi machine, digs around in the slot marked RETURN.

"Zilch," she says. "Patience and fortitude." (Fyorty-toot. Ask Michel, if I ever see him again. Not that I want to.)

"I love you," he says.

"You're sweet," she answers back. She seems to be deciding which way to go and, at the same time, without turning around, scouting out the territory to make sure her leather boys can't waylay her.

She smacks his bottom with a featherlight hand. "It's not far," she says.

A stretch of wasteland, a metal fence around a jail, or maybe a school, a mountain of beer cans, half-naked children trying to lasso each other with electric cables. An enormous barracks. Arrows, names, circles scrawled all over the walls in chalk. Stairs. I won't count them. The fourth floor. She has narrow hips. "I love you, Rachel."

"I know," she says, and pushes against an unpainted door that seems to be jammed at the bottom. Just as Jake is about to brace his shoulder against it, the door flies open; there was a squashed pack of cigarettes in the way.

"Silly Jeff," she says.

The smell of ammonia, cats, and puke is overwhelming. She walks across the room, pushes open a door, and leaps, like a child, onto a metal bed that creaks and squeaks.

"Wait," he says.

"I can't wait," she says hoarsely.

"I'll give you ten dollars extra."

She comes back into the room with the bare walls and scattered belongings: car tires, lead pipes, a crate full of pocket mirrors, the handlebars of a motorcycle. On the mantelpiece, next to a framed photograph of a soldier, is a roast chicken made of amber-colored cardboard.

He squeezes himself into a narrow armchair. She leans against a table, on top of which are a bread knife, an electric drill, a saw, and a pile of wood shavings. Through the grimy windowpanes Jake can see the shadow of a tower.

"I don't get too many foreigners," she says, pulling off her fur jacket. "Foreigners don't like me."

(In this room, up close, she seems younger. I don't want to guess.)

"You're so quiet," she says. "Talk to me."

She lets go of the table and kneels down next to a wobbly little buffet, gets back up again, groaning, with a hip flask. The stuff inside tastes even worse than the whiskey in Rev'em-up Red's porcelain Harley.

"Moonshine," she says, her strange face crinkling into a smile. "I used to have real nice furniture. Used to. But Jeffie sold everything when I went to jail. For possession." She points to the picture, gazes at it wonderingly, tenderly. "That's Joe, my husband. He looks like you."

The soldier couldn't be more than thirty. He has struck a cheerful pose, yet there's something suspicious in the gaze that looks like Rachel's, steady and clear. "Killed in Nam," she says. "On his last leave he made a bench. Redwood. Fantastic. What's your name?"

200

"Jacob," says Jacob.

"You a Jew?" (Joo? What's that?) Jake nods. Wild guess.

"I knew it the minute I saw you," she says, she lies.

"I have a daughter," he says. "She's a little sick in the head. I don't know what to do. My wife too. Maybe she should go to a mental home, where they can take care of her, but I heard the girls in those places always have to play maid." He speaks each word slowly, carefully. (I can speak it better than I can understand it.)

"Gene Tierney had a daughter like that," she says. "She was playing tennis one day with a bunch of other celebrities when she was four months' pregnant, and this woman, one of the crowd there watching who adored her because she was so gorgeous, and very sophisticated, asked her for her autograph and hugged her, and five months later Gene Tierney had a deformed kid. You following me? And later on she met that same woman at a cocktail party and the bitch said she knew her, she'd met her once on a tennis court, only at the time she wasn't really allowed to leave the house because she had smallpox. Women like that should be strangled. Can you imagine, *crucifying* a great star like Gene Tierney!"

A sink in the corner starts gurgling. "Shit," she says. The smell of ammonia grows stronger. (Why haven't I sent my father a postcard? He just sits there all day stuffing himself with almond cakes. Only Uncle Leo ever comes to visit him, and they play cards, but he can't even see the cards anymore, Uncle Leo usually lets him win. Worked all his life in the gas plant. The slow death, they call it there. The folks who live around the gas plant are nervous wrecks. Always fighting, like cats and dogs.)

"You're fat," she says. "That's bad for you."

"I get it from my father. He eats till he breaks. I mean, bursts."

"I'm never hungry," she says. (She suddenly remembers why I'm here and gives me a voluptuous pout that makes her look like that dancer who looked like her.) "Not for food, anyway," she says with a whorish drawl.

"Cut it out," grumbles Jake.

"Whatcha got in the bag? A present for me?"

She burst out laughing when she sees the cans of beans. Why? She takes out Rev'em-up Red's motorcycle. "That's cute."

"Porcelain," he says.

"No," she says. She goes into the bedroom and returns with a plate, points to a pair of blue crossed swords. "*This* is porcelain. Meissen. Onion pattern, dinnerware." (Can't follow this, can't translate it.) "From Joe's grandmother." (That, I understand.)

Compared to the delicate little plate, the motorcycle, which he thought was such a work of art, looks like something from a dime store. Jake feels ashamed. His eyes burn. ("Get up, you stupid fuck! That goddamn bawling of yours the whole time . . .")

"You ready to screw me now?"

Jake pulls four five-dollar bills out of his pocket, then two more.

"Another two," she says. "You won't be sorry." She rolls up the money and slips it in her blouse.

"My wife," says Jake, "comes from the poor side of Merelbeke. That's why she's always kept after Didi, my daughter Didi. Sent her to special classes, extra math lessons, piano. Because she wanted Didi to be more than *she* was. Understand, Rachel?" She nods.

"I bought her a present. Liver pâté, specially made in England for the Queen's Silver Jubilee. Queen Elizabeth."

"What's your queen like over there in Belgium? Is she friendly?"

"Yes, very nice," says Jake.

"Does she love her husband, the prince?"

"He's not a prince, he's a king."

"Well, well," she says. Jake is having more and more trouble following her English. (I've got to pay attention. Got to listen. But I can't.)

"We should strangle 'em, the whole bunch, all those fucking princes and kings, shitty bastards. Send their kids to the Salvation Army or a shelter, just like they did to us."

(That's one thing the Americans will never understand, what it means to have a king. Rickabone explained it to me once: It's not the person that matters, Jacob, it's the concept. The concept of power that can never be bought, not with votes, not with violence, not even with money.)

"Monsters, all of 'em. Shit, the government, that's the *real* enemy," she says.

A bony young man walks in. He's wearing a leather apron with no shirt underneath. Above his right elbow, in sea-blue letters, is the word MOM. "Has he paid yet?" he asks.

"Yeah. Can't you see I'm busy?" she says, but not sharply enough. The boy picks up the drill, fiddles with the bit.

"Did you do her with this?"

"No," says Jake. Sleep comes over him in persistent little waves, watery fingers around his eyebrows. Did Rachel put something in that awful drink?

"Keep your fucking hands off my drill," says the boy, "or I'll screw this nozzle in your schnozzle." He storms back into the bedroom and flings himself down on the metal bed, so hard it makes the cardboard chicken wobble on the mantlepiece. Jake hears the rustling of a newspaper.

"He means well," says Rachel. "He just got discharged from an institution. He couldn't get used to it. Too much greasy food." (Wheezy prude?)

"A person can get used to anything, except peace and happiness, you bitch!" screams the boy.

(And desire. What's the American word for that? I've got to know.) Jake asks her.

"Want?" he says. "To want? The word for want?"

"You want it? You'll get it," she says with a fruity laugh.

"I feel want," he says, laying his hand on his heart like an opera singer on TV. (My desire is like a boxing match that starts up again each morning, a two-fisted bout with being alone, with being left alone, with the unimaginable weariness I'm feeling right now.)

"American word for want," he says. In the bedroom, the boy flings his newspaper against the wall. He stands in the doorway, his hair sticking out all over his head like stalks of beach grass. A mildly amused and wicked grin appears on his pointed face.

"Dee-*zey*-yuh," he says. "That's the American word. Right?" He has his mother's eyes.

"Thank you."

"Jeffie's a whizz at crosswords," says Rachel tenderly. The boy picks up the porcelain Harley. Jake wrests the cool, fragile bottle from the bony fingers. Jeffie immediately assumes his most threatening stance, legs spread, back arched.

"Go to sleep, you shit!" barks Rachel. (Jeffie's the Paradise Strangler, I'm sure of it.)

204

Jeffie sits down on the edge of the armchair, reeking of sweat and motor oil, and puts his arm around Jake's shoulder. "You an' me," he says. Rachel starts cursing at him in a rapid, incomprehensible, vaguely German-sounding language. Jeffie answers just as vehemently in the same language. Jewish. Joo. Joe.

"Come on," says Rachel. Jake follows her, down the stairs. She clings to the banister like an old woman. "He's got the wrong friends," she says. "If only Joe were here . . ." she mumbles.

Outside, in the terrifyingly white sunlight, she looks ridiculous, like a scarecrow, with one arm pointing to a windowless shed.

"Let's get it over with," she says grumpily.

(Way up in the sky, between the white sun and this wasteland, a satellite with electronic monitoring devices is slowing down above our heads, its high-power lenses aimed right at us.)

Rachel pushes open the aluminum door and goes over to a car with no tires. ("What kind of car?" Staf van't Peperstraatje is going to ask me. An Oldsmobile. Old enough to have made its First Communion.) She pushes the seat up and falls sideways onto the back seat, which is strewn with flat square cushions. Jake tries to squeeze in beside her, but doesn't fit. Gasping for breath, he crawls behind the steering wheel, where he can barely move. Dead tired, his eyes on the dashboard, he says, with a sigh that sticks in his powder-dry throat, "I love you."

"Shit," says Rachel. She sits up, gives his shoulder a nudge, and climbs halfway over the back of the seat. The weight of her body presses him forward but he pushes off against the wheel as she, with shaking, determined fingers, unbuttons his fly.

"Fuckin' liar," she says, "you're no Jew!" and plucks playfully at his foreskin. (Or did she say: You're not Joe, my warily smiling warrior of a lover of a man?) She tugs at his limp prick, it hurts.

Next to the dismantled car is a vending machine. *Ice Magic*, icicle letters.

"This won't work," she says.

They crawl, both breathing heavily now, out of the car. She kneels on the dusty cement floor, sinks down on one side, lies back and lifts up her dress. Jake peels off the three layers of stocking, down to her calf. Her skin is light purple.

"Bad circulation," she says, scratching his head. "Don't worry," she says. "I haven't had the clap in years. Come on. Patience and fortitude." She laughs, flashes her magnificent teeth, the rippling white expanse of her belly, the woolly triangle, the thick, lilac lips.

"What's wrong?" she asks.

"Willingly," says Jake.

"I will if you will, lover," she says, "and I know what you want." She gropes around on the floor and throws a rag, oilstained and smelling faintly of gas, over her face.

"Lover," says her muffled voice under the rag, which she pats carefully around her nose and chin. Jake snatches it off. Transfixed by her clear, unwavering gaze, he stares into the opal ovals, the aquamarine pupils of the angel he struck dead, and plunges into her smooth, warm, slippery depths. "Darling Jacob," says Rachel.

He wakes to the sound of a train thundering past, the Ice Magic machine softly clattering, and a voice saying, "Mister, Mister, you forgot something."

Jeffie, now in a jean suit, hands him his plastic bag. "Mom's asleep," says Jeffie. "The sleep of the just."

Jake fishes the porcelain motorcycle out of the bag and gives it to the boy. "Come back soon," says Jeffie, winking.

"Yes, sir," says Jake. What he meant to say was, "Yes, boy."

At half past ten his cab pulls up in front of the motel. Michel is sitting in the lobby eating a huge bowl of ice cream speckled with phosphorescent chunks of candied fruit. "You're right on time," says Michel, subservient, dangerous. "I was just about to call the police."

24

As for me, the clown who's been telling you all this, sir, like you're one of the Unicorn family, I've got my own thoughts about it, about the journey those two made, but who am I to go shouting them from the roof of the Gravensteen?

We still see Michel at the Unicorn every now and again. He's not the same Michel he used to be. They say Travel Broadens the Mind, but goodness knows what it did to Michel's! We don't snub him, of course, at least not outright. But ever since those two came back from the Promised Land and we never saw our old pal Jake anymore, Michel isn't welcome here. Not really. 'Cause even though we don't know the whole story, we all know it must've been his fault that the very same week they came home, Jake moved out of town.

The minute Michel walked into the Unicorn, about three days after they got back, we knew he'd changed. We swamped him with silly questions, just to wipe that frown off his face. There were so many, he couldn't answer 'em all.

No, he hadn't seen any Indians.

Yes. Cowboys, he'd seen. But not on horseback.

And those Hormones out in Utah, those polygamists, those filthy prickamists?

None of them, either.

Did they get laid? What did it cost? Was it true the women in America went crazy if they didn't come every three minutes?

Michel looked at us like we were a bunch of dancing bears.

"Aw, come on, Michel, tell us," we begged. "What did you play? How much did you lose? Did you ever hit the jackpot, or at least see somebody else do it?"

"How about Jake?" asked Salome.

"Jake?" said Michel. "He didn't behave himself very well."

"What do you mean?"

Michel scooped up that old fleabag of a Mister Jules, set him on his lap, and let him drink from his glass of stout.

"You'll have to ask him that yourself," he said.

Now we're not the sort of folks that'll grill a fellow when he doesn't feel like talking. So we didn't press the point.

That evening Michel watched over our shoulders as we played. After a while he said, "Yup, they play differently in America."

"Then why don't you just turn around and go right back," snapped Felix the Sourpuss, his prissy little moustache twitching.

"Think I'd like it there, over in America? Think I should go?" asked Deaf Derek, laying down a full house.

"Sure. Just don't forget the bankroll," said Michel.

"Are the casinos over there classier than here? What I mean is, can a working guy like me get in?" asked Staf van 't Peperstraatje, who's a Socialist.

"Anybody can get in," said Michel. "Makes no difference who you are. They may be kind of loud, those Americans, but everyone gets equal treatment."

When Michel is nervous he lisps and swallows his words, like that fellow who lies about the weather on TV. Of course, he's not as jovial as the weatherman, he's more of a pompous bastard. Because you'll have to admit, sir, it's downright arrogant, just because you've hopped on a plane and spent ten days in America, to cast doubt on the democracy of the Unicorn! Just to give you an example: you can walk in here any day and see the mayor of Vijve Sint Elooi playing cards with a window washer. Though come to think of it, the mayor'll play with *anybody* if he gets the chance.

Later that night Michel said, "I brought you a present," and he gave Verbist the Schoolmaster a *Penthouse*, one which hadn't been mauled by the Belgian government.

"Why *thank* you, sir," said Verbist the Schoolmaster in that fancy English he learned at school, and after he was done drooling over it, we were allowed to flip through. What a pleasure! No inkblots or splotches of acetone defiling the brushwood, you could see the mice for what they were. Everyone was satisfied.

All except Markie, that is, who, as I've already said, hates Michel's guts. When Salome and Doctor Verbraeken had their backs turned he stuck out his tongue at Michel. Markie-the-Kid! Michel didn't seem to notice. So Markie, just to rile him, started singing that song *"Michelle, ma belle,"* the one the Beatles were always wailing over the radio. That's when he walked out, Michel did. And for all I care, he can stay out. But if he'd rather keep hanging around, we're not going to lose any sleep over it, because he does come in handy now and again, if you want to get a good deal on a TV, for instance, or a Xerox machine. But we can't say we're thrilled to see him.

Where's Jake living now? A village in Limburg. Wanted to be closer to his daughter, who's in a mental home out there. Seems that while he was off in America she suddenly took a turn for the worse. Helène at the Saint Tropez told us that Didi had begun stuffing her mouth with toilet paper, and her nostrils, and her ears, and *you know where*—in short, plugging up all her holes.

Still, it's strange that Jake never even came to say goodbye. We're not going to shed any tears over it, but it does feel odd when you forget yourself in the heat of the game and call out to Patrick, "Three pints!" or "What'll it be, Jake?" and he isn't there, in his spot beside the bar, our gentle Flemish giant.

Would you look at that, it's hailing outside! No matter, we're warm and dry in here, eh, sir? Whatever happens out there, it's no concern of ours. The weather is just like the government: you can't do a thing about it. Isn't that true? Look, Mister Jules is wagging his tail. He agrees.

Patrick! A Worthington stout for Mister Jules!